Y0-ABV-964

"This feels good, doesn't it, Charly? Would it kill you to admit I could do something for you?" J.D. asked as he massaged the tight muscles of her neck.

"I'm doing this against my will," she muttered.

"I know, I know, I'm holding you captive. Relax, Charly, you've had a long day." His fingers moved to her shoulder blades, his thumbs to her spine. He massaged and rubbed until her head fell forward. He circled her back gently, then pulled her shirt from her jeans and slid his hands underneath. He stroked and caressed her, but his hands trembled as they curved around her waist and pressed upward.

Suddenly he stopped, and Charly turned bewildered eyes to him, eyes smoky with the same desire her body had lit within him.

"Don't you just want to be friends?" she whispered.

He took her hand in his, kissed her fingertips slowly, and pressed her palm against his chest. Surprise lit her eyes as she felt the wild rhythm of his heartbeat. "Does that feel like the heart of a man who just wants to be friends?"

She jerked her hand back in shock.

J.D. smiled. "Hide your head in the sand all you want, Charly. But we will be lovers. . . ."

WHAT ARE *LOVESWEPT* ROMANCES?

They are stories of true romance and touching emotion. We believe those two very important ingredients are constants in our highly sensual and very believable stories in the *LOVESWEPT* line. Our goal is to give you, the reader, stories of consistently high quality that may sometimes make you laugh, sometimes make you cry, but are always fresh and creative and contain many delightful surprises within their pages.

Most romance fans read an enormous number of books. Those they truly love, they keep. Others may be traded with friends and soon forgotten. We hope that each *LOVESWEPT* romance will be a treasure—a "keeper." We will always try to publish

LOVE STORIES YOU'LL NEVER FORGET
BY AUTHORS YOU'LL ALWAYS REMEMBER

The Editors

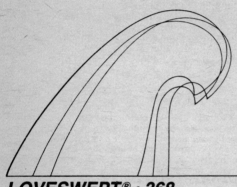

LOVESWEPT® • 368

Courtney Henke

The Dragon's Revenge

BANTAM BOOKS
NEW YORK • TORONTO • LONDON • SYDNEY • AUCKLAND

THE DRAGON'S REVENGE

A Bantam Book / December 1989

LOVESWEPT® and the wave device are registered
trademarks of Bantam Books, a division of
Bantam Doubleday Dell Publishing Group, Inc.
Registered in U.S. Patent
and Trademark Office and elsewhere.

All rights reserved.
Copyright © 1989 by Courtney Henke.
Cover art copyright © 1989 by Barney Plotkin.
No part of this book may be reproduced or transmitted
in any form or by any means, electronic or mechanical,
including photocopying, recording, or by any information
storage and retrieval system, without permission in
writing from the publisher.
For information address: Bantam Books.

If you would be interested in receiving protective vinyl
covers for your Loveswept books, please write to this address
for information:

Loveswept
Bantam Books
P.O. Box 985
Hicksville, NY 11802

ISBN 0-553-44002-0

Published simultaneously in the United States and Canada

Bantam Books are published by Bantam Books, a division
of Bantam Doubleday Dell Publishing Group, Inc. Its trademark, consisting of the words "Bantam Books" and the
portrayal of a rooster, is Registered in U.S. Patent and
Trademark Office and in other countries. Marca Registrada.
Bantam Books, 666 Fifth Avenue, New York, New York 10103.

PRINTED IN THE UNITED STATES OF AMERICA

O   0 9 8 7 6 5 4 3 2 1

For Keith, because it was his birthday; for Monalisa, because she laughed first; and for all the optimists of the world, because reality can be as good as fantasy.

One

Rats came in all shapes and sizes, but the wily beasts could learn a few lessons from a certain dainty, deceptively sweet old lady named Amanda, J. D. Smith thought as he watched painters hustle in and out of Rucker High School. He had to give his mother credit, though. For pure sneakiness she was unsurpassed.

J.D.'s generous mouth twitched in amusement. Amanda had nearly suckered the board of trustees into believing Rucker High School was a worthwhile cause. But they hadn't emotionally fenced with the woman for thirty-one years as he had.

His green eyes sharpened on the building as the setting sun illuminated every nook and cranny. The front and the leg of the first "R" in Rucker had been broken off so that the new name was hardly appropriate for any institution, and the coat of primer the painters had recently applied didn't hide the graffiti beneath the cracked brick walls. He understood now why Amanda had stalled the investigation with her ludicrous tales. J.D. had made it clear to her that her hopeless causes took too much of her charitable trust's budget—and this project demanded a good chunk. Obviously she'd gotten wind of his surprise visit and had decided to "pretty things up."

A spattered workman bumped into him, glanced up to excuse himself, then spared a second, astonished look before hurrying by. As J.D. checked his clothing for residue and tamed his unruly brown hair with an impatient hand, he didn't wonder at the man's surprise. In a neighborhood that had once been called "the war zone," he in his conservative three-piece suit stood out like a peacock among the sparrows. As he brushed apricot paint flakes off his sleeve, J.D. hoped this excursion wouldn't ruin his plans for the evening.

Striding to his left, he pulled his microrecorder out of his breast pocket and spoke into it as he walked around the building. "Nothing was allocated to chisel 'Rucker' in stone, Mother," he murmured wryly. "You must appreciate its present rather colorful name."

After stopping the tape, he paused in front of a graffiti-covered wall. One inventive limerick in particular caught his eye, and stifling a chuckle, he read it into the recorder.

As he rounded the corner of the building he heard male voices hooting in unison and saw a group of students racing across the field in formation, practicing drills. Football practice had started, he noted, even though the term didn't begin for three more weeks. He strode on, concentrating on his task. "This community consolidation project is laudable, Mother," he dictated, "but next time check your facts. You didn't do enough re—"

"Not so high!" someone yelled.

Something hit the wall beside him with a thud, and he instinctively crouched down—just before an electric-blue blur slammed into him.

His microrecorder went flying, and so did he, but reflexes honed by gruelling swordplay saved him from

major injury. As the sandy ground ꭇ‌ꭇ
meet him, he didn't fight the impetus of his ꭇ
He rolled with it, springing to his feet.

Behind him, he heard a violent series of coughs.
"Sunny beach!" a female voice spluttered. "Are
you—hurt?"

He turned to the blue-shirted woman who was
doubled over, choking. J.D. grabbed her, burying
his face in a wild mane of chestnut hair as he reached
around to place his fist in her diaphram.

"Don't—not the Heimlich maneuver!" she said between gasps, struggling in his arms. "I—busted my
ribs—years ago."

Since she could obviously breathe, J.D. hesitated,
then pulled out one hand and thumped her sharply
between the shoulder blades. She stilled for a moment, and he was suddenly aware that his palm
nestled beneath a very generous breast, that her
bottom fit snugly against him.

Footsteps thundered behind them. He ignored his
reaction and smacked her again. "I'm getting a
doctor."

"Hey, Dragon Lady! Hey, coach! Y'okay?"

"She's—"

"Don't—interfere," she managed to say, and peeled
his fingers from her chest.

"You need—"

"I'm fine!"

She tore herself away from him, and he caught a
glimpse of sky-blue eyes before she turned to the
line of tough-looking teenagers. Her spine straightened and her shoulders went back. He didn't know
which surprised him more, her imposing height or
her aggressiveness.

"Watch your altitude next time, Mendez." Her voice
was surprisingly steady as she addressed the boy.

J.D. stepped back with a frown. His gaze zeroed

in on her worn, nearly white jeans, which lovingly cupped her buttocks. He mentally cursed himself. The woman had practically choked to death, and he couldn't take his eyes off her backside!

"You sure you're okay, coach?" one player asked.

"I swallowed a triple-sized wad of chewing gum." She cleared her throat. "It's nothing a dose of drain cleaner won't cure."

"Dragons can eat anything," someone muttered.

"Watch it, Hogan." She chuckled and tossed the football out to them. "And so ends the demonstration on how *not* to catch a forward pass. Show's over! Get your playbooks!"

Everyone turned at once, and two players bumped together, glared at each other for a moment, then wandered away.

"Doesn't anybody ever watch where he's going around here?" J.D. murmured.

She spun around, a wicked grin curving her full mouth. "Sorry, people usually watch out for *me*."

J.D. caught his breath. So this was the freight train that had hit him!

A bright blue T-shirt proclaiming QUARTERBACKS MAKE BETTER PASSES was molded to an athletic, voluptuous frame that redefined the word "curve." Long chestnut hair laced with sere grass framed a makeup-free face. High, aristocratic cheekbones and an aquiline nose seemed at odds with her square jaw and stubborn chin.

She gave him an appreciative look. "Pretty fancy footwork back there. You recovered well for a business type." She stepped forward to brush dirt from his suit. "Ever play football?"

"No." He pulled away from her and continued the task himself. "I fence." The microrecorder lay at his feet, and he pocketed it.

"Fence? As in stolen goods or chain link?"

"Fence. As in swordplay."

"Funny, you don't look like the leotard type."

He'd heard all the jokes before and refused to rise to the bait. "And you don't look like a low-flying jet."

"Look closer," she muttered as she tucked her hands into her back pockets.

He couldn't help but look, yet it was her eyes that intrigued him. They were enormous, accented by lush, fly-away brows, and they were dancing with laughter. Yet something lurked in their depths, some trace of age-old wisdom and pain. Fencing had taught him to read his opponent with uncanny accuracy, but this woman was a mass of contradictions.

"You look familiar. Are you a reporter?" she asked.

"No." He tore his gaze away from her to glance at his watch, irritated at himself for forgetting his purpose. Though it was understandable. He didn't look forward to the job that lay ahead. "I have a meeting with your principal."

"David's here?" Speculation gleamed in her eyes for a moment, then she cocked her head. "Are you a new teacher?"

· "No:" He regretted that fact.

"Why don't you stick around?" she asked after a moment. "You'll never find David's office in that maze without a guide." She peeped at him from beneath full lashes. "Besides, you might learn something. About a *real* sport."

Before he could comment, she spun around and called for the team's attention.

"All right you guys! We'll skip the laps today, since I don't know if the plumbers have hooked the showers back up."

A cheer greeted this pronouncement.

"Don't get used to it," she went on. "It's just for today. Study those playbooks and keep 'em safe! Watch for your openings, and be prepared to take 'em. Mendez, accuracy! Hogan, get a rein on that temper of yours, or you'll be easy prey for the offensive line. This is a game, not a gang war!

"Remember this, everybody! The minute you let your personal feelings get in the way, the minute you give your opponent that edge, you're predictable. And the minute you become predictable, you've lost the game."

J.D. frowned. Her philosophy was remarkably similar to his eccentric and manipulative family's. Too bad, he thought.

Charly watched the team wander away, scowling over the first day's practice. Tempers were running too high, she realized. And if she couldn't straighten Hogan and Mendez out, she was in for major trouble.

Oh, well, she thought with a mental sigh. "Trouble" was her middle name, "strength" her key word. She'd been through much worse in her life, and the players respected her authority. As long as she could remain stronger than they, as long as she could beat them with her inherent humor, she could do anything.

Automatically, she groped for her whistle, then remembered it was missing. She glanced around the barren ground. Beside the building, beneath a perpetually leaking faucet, a tiny purple-and-white lupine struggled for life. It reminded her of her football team. In desolation, something wonderful always emerged.

"Is this what you're looking for?"

She turned, having forgotten about the stranger in her musings. He stood just behind her, holding out an object in his palm.

Why did he look so familiar? Though he still bore traces of their tumble, his green eyes showed no trace of any emotion. And he he held himself as if he had no idea that his expensive, conservative suit looked ready for Goodwill. The man had class, she thought, and that indefinable something that indicated command.

A shiver traveled down her spine.

"My whistle," she said.

"The chain broke." He dangled it upside down from his fingertips when she made no move to take it. "Probably in the collision."

Charly couldn't take her eyes from his hand. Muscle and sinew were clearly defined. He was probably built like a rock under that suit, and he had the reflexes of a cat. Something that had long been dormant stirred within her, but she tamped it down. "Thanks," she said, taking the whistle from him. "Clapping and yelling can be exhausting."

"You're the coach."

She nodded, crossing her arms over her chest. "Are you surprised?" she asked.

J.D. raised one imperious brow. "Should I be?"

"I hate people who can do that! Mine both go up." She demonstrated. "See? I just can't seem to get the hang of it."

He shrugged. "It's genetic."

She nodded solemnly. "That's what my mom used to say. I can't wiggle my ears either." She sighed. "Life is hard."

Was it her imagination, or did his green eyes darken and focus on her chest? Her breasts tingled as though he had touched her there. She spun from him, confusion clouding her judgment. She didn't even know him, for heaven's sake! And she didn't want to.

"The office," he reminded her.

She pasted a smile on her face. "Follow me," she called over her shoulder as she strode toward the building.

Charly headed for the nearest door, the one she always left unlocked so the team had access to the bathroom, and reached for the knob. A strong hand got there first. Startled, she glanced up into faintly mocking eyes. "Allow me," he said, and pulled.

Nothing happened. Stifling a grin, Charly kicked the lower edge and hip-slammed the middle. Then she waved him on. This time the door opened, and she preceded him into the building, jerking the crashbar tight to lock it behind them. "Chivalry isn't dead, huh?" she murmured with a cheeky grin.

"Fencing is the last of the chivalrous sports."

There was a touch of dry humor in his voice. Charly liked that quality in him. "Chivalrous?" she asked. "Or chauvinist?"

"Women compete all the time."

"Ah, but against themselves, or against men?"

"Themselves."

She nodded firmly. "Chauvinist."

"But I would never stop a woman from going *against* me. Can you say the same for football?"

She raised both brows. "I amend my statement." Her eyes narrowed. "Sexist, not chauvinist."

He stifled a tiny smile. "I'll be certain to avoid a match with you."

She chuckled and waved him forward. The smell of wet paint made her wrinkle her nose as they wandered the maze of hallways toward David's office. His ease with repartee exhilarated her, she realized as they walked, yet his conscious repression of humor confused her.

"This is it," she said, and pounded on the unmarked door once before entering. "David, you have a visitor."

At first David appeared to be startled, then he grinned. At least she thought he did. She could never tell what was going on beneath that mangy, silver-streaked bush he called a beard. "Don't you ever knock?"

It was an old, running argument. She pretended affront. "I did!"

"Just before you waltzed in."

"Why should I ruin my record?"

David's gaze traveled to J.D., and apprehension clouded his features. He raked one hand through his dusty blond hair, using the other to straighten his tie.

David? In a tie? Good grief, who was this man she'd shown in?

"Mr. Smith, I'm happy to meet you at last."

As the men greeted each other Charly frowned. She hadn't seen David so nervous since . . . she couldn't remember *ever* having seen him so nervous. "David?" she asked softly, her protective instincts leaping to the fore.

"Won't you be seated?" he told the stranger, then he hurried over to Charly. "Go put your equipment away," he said.

Glaring at him, Charly answered back, "The team is taking care of it."

A pleading light filled the eyes of a man who'd been more of a father than her own. "Charly—"

"What's wrong?" she whispered. "Who is that?"

"J. Derek Smith. He holds the purse strings on one of the biggest charitable trusts on the West Coast. Remember Amanda?"

"That odd little old lady who came by last week?"

He nodded. "His mother."

No wonder he looked so familiar, she thought. She had barely spoken to the other woman, but she had been memorable. "But David—"

"Mr. Bakker, can we get on with this? I have another appointment."

"I've got a bad feeling about this," she murmured as David closed the door on her. If this was about David's precious community consolidation, she had a horrible feeling he was dead in the water. And she had delivered the executioner!

Charly pressed her ear against the panel.

". . . Though the gang wars ended years ago," she heard David say, "my job isn't finished. I propose to establish a network of community, parental, and student involvement."

"Right on," she whispered. "Get 'em, David." Though she had very little to do with his project, David was usually right. Lord knew he'd proven that to her over the last twelve years.

"My hands are tied with the present system," David went on. "I can only do so much here, and it's just not enough. I want to break the cycle."

She heard the other man murmur a response, but couldn't understand his words. Frowning, she turned the knob slowly, carefully, and the door opened a crack. She could hear no better, but she couldn't widen the slit without its becoming noticeable. Crouching, she craned her neck to listen.

The door opened.

Charly glanced up into cool green eyes. She straightened quickly, surprised to find she still had to look up at him. Why hadn't she noticed how tall he was before?

"Waiting for someone?" he asked in a dry tone.

"Godot?"

He looked startled for a moment, then his face went blank. "He's not coming."

"He never does." She cleared her throat. "Finished already?"

"Yes." He nodded once, then strode down the hall toward the main entrance.

"Hey!" she called, but he disappeared around a corner.

David walked out of his office looking defeated. "Charly, what are you still doing here?"

"You weren't in there long." Her hopes sank. "David, what happened?"

"Well . . . ," he said heartily, but he wasn't able to relate the bad news. "The building is secure. Be sure and use the side door—the front is chained. I'm on my way out," he stated, turning to leave.

Her heart twisted with David's pain. "You didn't get it," she whispered.

David sighed. "Charly, I didn't have any time. His foundation . . ."

"Turned you down," she supplied.

His shoulders slumped. "Yeah." He sighed again. "I knew it was too early."

"But you presented it anyway."

"I had to. He called me a couple of hours ago. I thought we'd have a week at least. But he wanted to see it right away."

"That—" Indignation filled her, and her chin tilted up. She knew something David didn't, and it was an opening she could use. "I'll see you tomorrow, David." She rushed toward the main doors.

"Charly, where are you going? They're chained."

"Just some business! See you tomorrow!"

She glanced behind her long enough to ascertain that David was indeed leaving, then she broke into a run. She found her quarry staring in frustration at the padlocked chain strung through the crashbars on the double-doored main entrance.

"Mr. Smith!"

He glanced up, then strode past her. She tried to catch his arm, but he was too fast. "Wait a minute! I want to talk to you!"

"There's nothing to talk about."

"Dammit, stop!" He didn't, but she did and stamped her foot. "I owe the cuss bucket a dollar, and it's all your fault."

He froze. "The what?"

She slipped around in front of him, grinning. "The cuss bucket. The language can get pretty blue here."

His smile warmed the cool green of his eyes to the color of summer leaves and spread slowly into shallow dimples. Charly could only wonder why she'd thought breathing a necessary function in the past. She didn't seem to need it now.

"Make much money?"

"Enough for a VCR," she muttered, tearing her gaze away. Holy cow! It took an act of will to remember why she'd stalled him. "But not enough to fund the community consolidation."

His smile faded. "I'm sorry, Ms. . . . ?" He raised an inquiring brow.

"Charly."

"Just Charly?"

She shrugged, holding her hands wide. "My last name is this long and mostly consonants. I doubt if you could spell it, much less pronounce it."

"I really am sorry. But it's just not enough to have a worthwhile project." Then he spun on his heel and strode away.

"Hey!" Charly followed, determined to make him listen or at least to see that spark of amusement in his eyes again. "Mr. Smith, David's project is more than worthwhile! He wants to incorporate the youth centers and the shelters under one organization, to—"

"I read the proposal." J.D. paused, then turned down a branching corridor. He didn't seem to realize it was the wrong way. "Mr. Bakker is an admirable principal, but he's not ready to take on something this big. It's too ambitious."

Anger rose inside her. "Then tell him how to fix it!"

J.D. stopped. She crashed into him, her soft breasts cushioning the blow. He swallowed hard.

Bracing himself mentally, he drew himself up to his full six feet five inches and turned.

His heart beat faster as he looked down into her proud face. She was open, honest, and outspoken, despite her weird theories on football. He could see it all in those features.

She began to speak again, and he began to feel trapped by her and her ageless eyes. He owed no one an explanation, and he was a fool to even consider it. "My decision is final."

He turned and pulled at the nearest unmarked door. Nothing happened.

"If you would just listen!" she said as she reached around him and slapped the door, then jerked it open for him. He stepped inside before he realized his mistake.

"The ladies' room," she told him.

He gave her a dark look and stalked away. "No kidding." He strode to the next one, tried it, found it stuck, too, and kicked it. It opened, he stormed in.

"Mr. Smith—"

All he could see was a short hallway, and he advanced knowing she'd follow close behind. Beyond it was a small, white room. There were two doors on the left, a high, barred window in front of him, and three cots, folded blankets at their feet, along each wall.

"The nurse's office," she said.

Holding his temper with difficulty, he retraced his steps and tugged at the door. Nothing happened. He kicked it. Nothing. He rattled the knob. No good.

"It's locked," he said ominously.

And he had a horrible suspicion this "open and honest" woman had orchestrated the whole thing.

Two

Charly gave him a withering look and reached past him for the doorknob. She rattled it, but it didn't open. Frowning, she kicked the bottom of the jamb and tried again. Nothing. "It's stuck," she told him.

"No kidding."

His faintly mocking tone irritated her. She slammed her shoulder into the door, but came away with only a bruise.

"It opens in," he said drily, and she narrowed her eyes. Grasping the knob tightly, she planted one foot to the side and pulled. Her hand slipped and she crashed into him.

He steadied her, the scent of his cologne wrapping around her as tightly as his arms. Her stomach lurched, and she tore out of his grasp, rubbing her aching muscles. "You want out so badly, do it yourself!"

"I can't do any worse than you. Haven't you heard of finesse?"

She huffed, then decided he was baiting her. "Sure. It's a cream rinse, right?"

14

He crossed his arms over his chest, eyeing her appraisingly. "You did this purposely, didn't you?"

"Yeah, I love pain. It's good for the soul."

"I mean, you sent me on that wild-goose chase to the front doors, then tricked me in here and locked the door."

"I chased you. And it locked by itself." She grinned wickedly. "But as long as we're here—"

"I knew it!" He pointed an accusing finger at her. "You wanted to talk to me, and now you have a captive audience."

"I know when to take advantage of an opening. There's a difference."

"It's just a little too convenient."

She shook her head, astonished by his reasoning. "Lord, you have a suspicious mind."

"Yes, I do. With good reason."

"You're nothing like your mother."

"Why doesn't it surprise me that you know each other?" He gave the door one last jerk. "I don't believe this," he muttered. "You probably battered it tighter with that little performance."

"Me?" Charly placed her hands on her hips. "If anyone's to blame, it's you! You were the one who just rushed in. Don't you ever *walk* anywhere?"

"Not when I'm trying to escape someone."

"If you'd have listened in the first place—"

"Stop!" He threw up his hands. "Call."

"Time out?"

"Whatever. Can we just worry about getting out? I'm sure we can fight later with no pause for breath."

"Oh, I don't know." Charly smiled in triumph, confident that this situation would work to her advantage. With them thrown together, he'd *have* to listen to her. Where would he go? "I kind of like it here. It's cozy." She caught a fleeting glimpse of amusement in his eyes, but it was gone quickly.

Why did he fight to be so austere? "Loosen up! It's not so bad in here. We have a place to sleep, sunshine, what more could anyone ask for?"

"Oh, I don't know. Food? Freedom from pestering females?" He strode to the other room, to one of the two doors and rattled it.

"That leads to the main office. It's always locked." When he moved to the other and jerked it open, she grinned. "Bathroom!" She waved to it as if it were a treasure house. "See? We even have water and, er, facilities."

"If they work." He turned on the faucets. "They do." He tried the light switch. "But no electricity."

"So? Who needs it? We can indulge in the good, old-fashioned lost art of conversation." When he glared at her, she grinned. "You're stuck with me."

"Thanks to my mother," he muttered.

"What's that supposed to mean?"

"She gave your principal the money for these renovations!"

Charly gave a short bark of laughter. "Wrong again, O ye of little faith. This is standard procedure before school opens. Do you expect us to *leave* it like this indefinitely?"

"Oh. It doesn't matter anyway. We're still trapped." He studied the room. "What about the window?" He climbed atop the cot against the wall and examined the casement. "Aha!" With a triumphant cry, he slid it open.

"In case you haven't noticed, it's barred. Do you happen to have a hacksaw on you?"

He shook the solid steel, then turned and sat on the edge of the cot. "Sorry," he said drily. "I left it in my other suit."

"A joke! Ha!" He glared at her again, and she giggled unrepentantly. "I love a disgruntled man with a sense of humor," she said. "Come to think of it, I love a man with a sense of humor period."

"I don't have one of those either." His mouth twitched, as if he were holding back his amusement with effort, which confused her to no end. "There must be a way out of here."

"Why don't you just make the best of it?"

"I don't give up easily."

"Neither do I, but I know when to drop back and punt." Charly curled up on the floor, her back against the cold concrete wall. It appeared that she would have a long time in which to plead David's case, and she had to, as much for her kids as for David. She could afford a little patience, especially since her persistence only seemed to irritate him. She'd find the right opportunity. She always did. "Sit down."

"You're not going to help, are you?"

"Are you asking?"

"No."

"I didn't think so," she muttered. Funny, she thought, he was doing exactly what she would do if their positions were reversed. "Tell me if you find a hidden tunnel or something."

He didn't deign to answer her, and she didn't blame him.

As he continued to prowl the room he stripped off his suitcoat, revealing a hard, lean build. Her pulse picked up speed. She'd been right about one thing, at least. Beneath his shirt, strong muscles rippled with his every movement. Though not massive, he exuded the kind of power she associated with the big cats—pure, coiled energy. Though he paced restlessly back and forth, searching for a way out of their cage, there was no wasted movement, no excess labor to slow him down. The man was solid, capable—and dangerous to her peace of mind.

Ruthlessly, she buried those odd feelings he stirred.

In her experience strong men only complicated things. *Any* man complicated things. "Relax. Somebody'll come along. Eventually."

"David?"

"He's long gone."

"The police? They'll see my car."

"Anything's possible. But don't get your hopes up."

"The janitor?"

"Sorry. Off until repairs are finished."

"Then who in the heck do you think will come?"

She shrugged and peeped at him from beneath her lashes. "Why are you in such a hurry?"

J.D. wondered about that himself but felt trapped. After labeling her honest and outspoken, he felt like a heel for suspecting that she had orchestrated this scenario, especially after she'd explained about the renovations. But after living with Amanda—and everybody else in his family—everyone became suspect. And something told him that Charly and Amanda were soulmates in spite of their slightly different outlooks. He would never make the same mistake his father had, he would never become involved with anyone he couldn't understand, with whom he couldn't share his goals and views.

He was grabbing at any excuse to allay his attraction to her, he realized, wondering why the woman had the ability to make him think in terms of an involvement. In any event, he knew a way to break the spell. "I have a date tonight."

"Ah!" Cocking her head, she eyed his three-piece suit with her brows raised. "Let me see. She's around thirty, medium height, blond hair, of course. She wears skirts—knee length—but never jeans, her favorite food is chicken, she loves to sew, read, and go to the opera."

His spine stiffened as he met her amused gaze. "What are you doing?"

"Whiling away the time." She bit her lip in concentration. "She has money of her own but never asks you out, gives four hours a week to charity, and she wants the prerequisite two-point-three children." Her eyes narrowed. "And her name is . . . Elizabeth."

"Her name is Cheryl," he muttered, wondering why he couldn't seem to recall her face. "And her favorite food is chocolate."

Her blue eyes danced with delight. "I knew I'd have *something* in common with her. But I kicked the chocolate habit. I was getting fat."

"I can't imagine you being fat." J.D.'s voice dropped a tone. Startled by his own sentiment, he cleared his throat, heaved himself to his feet, and strode to the door. He wouldn't let himself become unbalanced! Getting out was their first priority. "We could hammer the pins out of the hinges!"

"With what? Our heads?"

He turned, frowning, and upended one of the three cots. "We could pull one of the legs off." He examined it, tapped it with the tip of his finger, then replaced it. "Rolled aluminum. We couldn't knock out a flea with that."

"Sure we could." Charly leaned her head back and closed her eyes. "Bring 'em on! We'll punch their lights out!"

"You're not helping!"

"What do you want me to do? Tear out the bars with my teeth?"

His silence stretched for long moments. "Empty your pockets."

Her eyes flew open. "What?"

He waved her up. "Just do it. Between us, we should have something we could use."

Sighing, Charly lifted her bottom off the floor and dug everything out of her pockets. J.D. did the same, and they heaped their treasures on top of a cot. Sitting at opposite ends, they both eyed the pile, she in amusement, he in disgust.

"Great," he said. "One microrecorder, abused." He tossed it aside. "One lip gloss."

"It's the lack of humidity," she said solemnly. "I chap."

His gaze zeroed in on her mouth, and she caught her breath. But he returned his attention to the stack. She didn't know whether to be disappointed or relieved.

He examined each item as if it held the secrets of the universe. "Two crumpled Safeway receipts . . ."

"There was a sale on grapes."

". . . one paper clip, one comb, a shopping list . . . hmm, no grapes. Impulse shopper, right?"

She shrugged. "I get cravings."

"One datebook, leather." She tried to peek at it, and he closed it quickly. "One checkbook, also leather." He frowned and studied it. "Could we make a lockpick out of the metal spiral?"

She raised both brows. "How would I know?"

"A maybe." He set it aside. "Two sets of keys, also maybes."

"Do you think I'd hold out on you?"

He eyed her for a moment. "No. But one of them might fit the door."

"Ah! You're a long-shot player."

"Two wallets—don't you carry a purse?—with approximately . . . thirty-four dollars between them, one rusty nail, sixty-three cents in change, and a ball of lint." He lifted one brow. "Did you really have to include that?"

"You said everything." Charly chuckled at his disappointed expression. "What did you expect? A magic wand?" She snapped her fingers. "I knew I should have followed my instincts. The first time I saw

MacGyver I should have bought myself a Swiss army knife just for emergencies."

"Wonderful." He went through the maybe pile again, holding up his key ring with a speculative look. Then he dropped it with a jingle and looked over at her. "I guess we'll have to spend the night together."

A frisson of panic rippled through her. She'd never spent the entire night with a man. She'd been afraid a true emotional relationship would deplete her somehow. Love had drained her mother, it would never have the opportunity to do the same to her. "I'll bet you send roses the morning after," she said with a sneer.

"Don't you like roses?"

"No." This was getting them nowhere. "If I try to get us out, will you listen to me?"

His eyes narrowed. "You do have a key."

"No." She picked up his wallet, forcing away her superstitious fear. "But you have something I don't." Brows raised, she removed a gold credit card. "You *really* have something I don't." She fanned herself with it. "You're loaded, right?"

"I'm not rich," he said firmly. "I run a bank."

"And what a bank!"

"I draw a salary just like everybody else."

She gave an unladylike snort. "Right. And the Amanda Smith fund just sprang up in your garden."

"My father left it to her."

"But it'll be yours."

He shook his head. "I have a say in the administration of the money, but she's the one who finds the charities. And believe me, she knows where to look. My father tried to tie everything up in legalities, but she's a smart lady. I seriously doubt if there will be anything left."

Though he gave her the opening she needed, his lack of bitterness intrigued her. It really didn't seem to bother him. "Oh, come on. I watch *Dynasty*, I know how you guys operate."

"It's her money!"

"Then why won't you let her give it to us?"

Charly watched as his hands clenched, fascinated by the play of emotions across his usually calm face. It made him more human, she decided, not knowing whether she liked that or not. "Are you going to strangle me?" she asked sweetly.

He struggled with himself. "No. Much as the idea appeals to me." After another moment his fist relaxed. "So, what are you going to do with my credit card? Eat it?"

"No." She glanced at the object in her hand, almost forgetting its function. In her experience, money tended to corrupt. Her father had been a prime example, but it hadn't been his only problem. And the lack of wealth hadn't caused her mother's heartache. The lack of her father had.

She forced her mind away from that line of thinking. "With any luck, I can use this to force the lock."

"I hope so," he muttered, and watched with interest as she stuck it between the door and the jamb easily. "Do this often?" he asked.

"Contrary to popular belief, we're not all thieves around here."

"That's not what I was implying."

She shot him a dark look, then went on with her task. After several minutes of jiggling, she growled and removed the card. "This sucker isn't moving at all." She handed it back to him. "Sorry."

He repeated her actions with no better results.

Charly sank to one cot, he to another across from her. "I guess we're stuck here for a while, huh?"

"I guess," he said softly.

Their gazes locked, and his green eyes warmed something deep inside her. Hurriedly, she looked away. She couldn't afford those softer emotions. Her only concern should be David, she told herself. "What should we talk about?"

"I don't know. The weather? The beautiful décor? I like white, don't you?"

"Mr. Smith—"

"J.D."

"J.D.," she said softly. "David's project is important to a lot of people."

"Let's not get into that again!"

" 'That' is exactly why we're here, remember?"

He sighed and paced to the window, examining the base of the bars. "Why the security? Drugs?"

"Needles, buster, needles! We have diabetics here, and we have to keep insulin on hand. What kind of misconceptions do you have anyway?" He said nothing, and frustration prompted her to add, "Great! We can add biased and closed-minded to the list of your better qualities."

His head snapped up. "That's a hell of a thing to say."

"But true! You made up your mind about us before you even came here, didn't you?"

"No. I have to retain a certain degree of objectivity. I did not predetermine this case based on anything I didn't understand."

Charly lifted her chin. "But you didn't even give David a chance to explain anything."

"He didn't need to."

"See?"

"I had facts and figures long before I met him."

"Papers! They're not people! They're not what make things work!"

"But they tell the story more clearly, with no distortions." He raised a brow. "And look who's talking about misconceptions! *Dynasty*, for pete's sake!"

Charly closed her eyes and fought her anger. This

would hardly help David's cause. "Okay. It wasn't exactly one of my better comments. But yours weren't much better!"

J.D. admitted the truth of that and wondered why he couldn't stop arguing with her. Her loyalty and her pride drew his admiration. After investigating charitable causes for more years than he cared to remember, he was used to the curious, even the determined attitudes of interested parties who tried to sway his decisions. But Charly's tactics went beyond anything he'd ever experienced—outside of what his family often did.

All of the Smiths had more heart than sense. He didn't like his job, but someone had to do it, and he just happened to have inherited more responsibility at nineteen, when his father had died, than anyone should have had to handle. Though he had always wanted to do more than just investigate the causes they dove into, someone had to straighten out their messes, to administrate. And he was good at it. The way Amanda schemed to throw her money away, he'd had to be.

Not for the first time in his life he wished he *could* get more involved. He'd seen more than his share of tragedy in the world, things that would make a stone weep, but he had to remain objective. Charly had been given choices in her life. He hadn't.

Lord, she was beautiful, he thought. Fury and accusation whirled in her blue eyes, stubbornness tightened her lips. Against his better judgment, his voice softened. "Charly, I admit it's a worthy cause. But all the good intentions in the world don't change facts."

Her nostrils flared, but she just nodded. "Go on."

J.D. fought the urge to kiss that defiant mouth. She wanted the truth? Unfortunately, she'd get it. "All right." He crossed his arms. "David's project is sloppy, and it would take more money than we have free at this moment to fix all the problems. We'd have to hire an administrator. There is no central controlling power, just a group of concerned citizens under an umbrella organization, and that is inefficient. His aim is laudable, but he has no focus. He has no way of tracking his money, and the funds he's applied for aren't necessarily used in the area where they're most needed."

"Which, in your expert opinion, is where?"

The edge of sarcasm in her voice stung. He'd lived with idealists far too long not to know the symptoms, and it aggravated him. "Why don't you try cleaning up your own act before tackling the entire community?" Relieved to see her expression harden, he went on. "Both the dropout and illiteracy rates at Rucker are still far above the national average. Do you have any kind of internship program? Job training? Remedial reading?"

"Of course we do!"

"But they're not effective. You could do far more with far less money right here in this school. You really want to help these kids? You want to give them a real chance? That's where you start. Not with a consolidation of existing programs, but an *enhancement*."

"What kind of ivory tower do you live in, Mr. Smith? Have you ever been into one of their homes to see the neglect? Your programs sound wonderful in theory, but they just don't cut it in the real world."

"They have cut it. Many times." J.D. could see the light of battle in her incredible blue eyes, and he sensed that she would defend David to the bitter end. "Let's just drop it, okay? I'm not closed-minded, but I refuse to argue about this. The decision has already been made."

"You are so stubborn!"

"I'm a realist, Charly."

"You're a pain in the—neck." She shoved her chestnut hair from her brow. "I'm not going to give up."

"Why?" He waved his arm. "This isn't even your fight. You're not involved at all."

"This is my school! These are *my* kids! It's clear that you don't know the first thing about this neighborhood."

"And you do?"

"I coach them, for heaven's sake!"

"Which doesn't explain why you're so interested. The sports program wasn't mentioned at all in the reports."

"I teach history too. I care about these kids."

Suddenly he saw old pain in the cloudy blue depths of her eyes. "It's more than that," he whispered. "Isn't it?"

Her gaze wavered, then dropped. "I owe David. I owe him more than you could ever understand."

"Are you and he—" He couldn't even voice his thought, and it stunned him that he'd even mentioned it.

She glared at him. "And you're dirty-minded on top of everything else! David Bakker is one of the most decent men I know. The only decent man it seems." Regret flashed in his eyes just for a moment. "He came to Rucker to fight a war that you'd never understand in a million years. He ended the gang wars that had plagued this neighborhood, and he did it single-handedly. But not by force. He"—her voice broke and she cleared her throat—"he outsmarted a seventeen-year-old girl into going to college by challenging her to an arm-wrestling match and winning. He talked a judge into sending a gang member into the army rather than jail. He stepped into more fights that I can count to take bloody kids to the hospital. He got *involved*. People do that, you know. They leave the paperwork behind them, and they give of themselves."

J.D.'s mouth hardened. "You have absolutely no concept of what I do for a living, lady."

"I know you care more about papers than you do about people. I know you worry about balance sheets and fiscal reports when you could *do* something."

His voice lowered to a dangerous purr. "I'm not going to defend myself to you, Charly. To you or anyone else."

"Because you can't!" She appraised him, her stance hostile. "You want to know what I owe David?" She jerked her T-shirt up. "This, Mr. Smith, is what I owe him."

Parallel to her waistline ran the faint etching of a scar. J.D. nearly cried out. "How—" He swallowed hard. "What did that?"

"A knife," she said bluntly, and turned to give him a better look. "I was in a gang once. A long time ago." She snapped the shirt down. "So you see, Mr. Smith, David saved my life. Because by making me go to college, by helping me get a scholarship, David gave me the chance you're denying them."

"You were that girl," he whispered, his heart aching for her.

She nodded. "I know these kids, J.D., because I was there once."

He reached out his hand and ran it over her ribs, feeling the imprint of her scar on his fingertips. Her skin warmed his palm, even through the fabric of her shirt. "Is this why you chose teaching?"

"That's part of it." Her eyes widened at his touch. "I wanted to help them somehow."

His gaze met hers, her pain almost visible between them. He slid his hand around her and pulled her close.

He hadn't meant to kiss her, but he had to wipe

the accusation from her eyes, to comfort and protect her from the nightmare she had lived. His lips brushed hers softly, driving the shadows from her face, and he found he couldn't stop there. With a sigh, he pressed his mouth to hers.

She shuddered and parted her lips. He accepted the invitation and touched her with his tongue, his pulse racing. His blood roared in his ears as he heard her tiny moan, as he felt her body melt against his.

She stiffened suddenly and tore herself from him. "Stop it! Don't you dare think you can ease your conscience by kissing me! I'm not one of your charities!" She spun on her heel and flew to the door.

"Charly!" J.D. fought with the chaos of emotions within him. He had not imagined his response, nor hers, but he didn't want it. He didn't want it!

He heard a slam and strode into the short hallway. Charly kicked the door again, growling in frustration.

With a cry, she pulled at the knob with all her might, and miraculously the door jerked open.

"Freedom!" he said, and returned for his jacket. Remembering his suspicions, he hurried back, expecting to see the door closed again. When he saw Charly lounging against the jamb, a hint of amusement curving her slightly swollen mouth, he relaxed. For a moment.

"Don't get too complacent, Mr. Smith," she told him. "I'm going to try and change your mind."

"You won't."

"But I'll keep trying."

J.D. wished things could be different between them. In another lifetime they might have been friends—or more. But now they were adversaries. He drew on his jacket and smiled wryly. "In fencing this would be called a standoff."

"In football we might go for sudden death."

He raised one brow and acknowledged her hit. "Right now I just want to go home."

"Down that hall," she said, and pointed. "All the way to the end."

He nodded and walked past her, resisted the urge to glance behind him. She was watching him. He could feel it.

"Watch your back," she called. "Now I have time to plan my strategy."

He didn't like the sound of that, he thought as he found the correct door. No, he didn't like the sound of that at all.

Three

"Mr. Smith?"

J.D. glanced up from his paperwork at his no-nonsense secretary, who stood just inside the doorway. "Yes, Miss Pickles?"

"The security guard has just informed me that your mother is on her way up." She smoothed her steel-gray hair in a nervous movement and flared her nostrils. "She's wearing a—" She cleared her throat, her mouth working as if she were trying to spit out a piece of gristle. "She's wearing a parachute, sir."

J.D. managed to keep his face blank. "Thank you, Miss Pickles. Show her in as soon as she lan—arrives."

Her chin lifted, and she glared down her bulbous nose. "Yes, sir."

After the door closed behind her, J.D.'s mouth widened in a grin that would have appalled the poor woman. In the last few days he'd found it difficult not to chuckle every time he said her name, and that had never happened in all the eleven years since his father's death. She looked like a pickle, he thought irreverently, all sour and lumpy. He seemed to remember his mother making a similar comment long ago, but as usual his father had shot her down with a disapproving scowl, and it had never come up again. But the long-standing feud between the two women had begun that day.

His smile faded. Three days ago he would never have indulged in such memories. He would have staunchly defended his father instead of seeing Amanda's side of it. But since then, he'd met Charly.

J.D. eased back in his leather chair, slipped his glasses off, and rubbed his eyes. Sleep had eluded him lately, and it was beginning to affect his work, his attitude. Charly's beautiful, paradoxical face had haunted his dreams since their night together. He wanted to hold on to his anger, but he couldn't. He wanted to remember his last glimpse of her, furious and stubborn, but he didn't.

Every time he closed his eyes he saw her impish expression, her vitality. And the previous night, to his horror, he had awakened in a sexual lather for the first time since he was fourteen. She had changed everything outrageously, and he had the sinking feeling that nothing in his life would ever be the same again—until he had purged her from his system.

And he would! He had to. He had seen firsthand how a woman like her could twist a man like him into knots. He knew exactly what he wanted in a wife, and the earthy Charly wasn't a candidate.

That he had even *thought* of her in terms of marriage disturbed him intensely. Anger he could hold on to, use to push her away. But those vulnerable blue eyes had gripped him as nothing else ever had. He had to clear her out of his mind once and for all. The question now was—how?

And why did he have the feeling she was just waiting for the perfect opportunity for a *riposte*, for her own attack?

He swore softly under his breath and found himself wondering if he had a dollar to cover it, then swore again out of sheer defiance. The woman was driving him crazy. His gaze drifted over his office, over the oak-paneled walls, the plush cream carpet, the priceless china vases filled with nothing but their own self-importance, and then he thought of battered lockers and potholed fields. And the laughing woman who had not only managed to take it all in stride, but to make it lovely.

With a mental shake he picked up his glasses and shoved them onto the bridge of his nose. Objectivity, he told himself firmly. It was none of his business anymore. But the tiny stack of papers in front of him only made him wish he wasn't so good at delegating authority. He was going to organize himself out of a job. He longed for a nice, meaty crisis to force his mind from thoughts of her rounded body.

As if some twisted fairy had decided to grant his wish, Amanda flung his door wide open at that moment. The oil paintings on the walls rattled.

"That woman," she muttered darkly, and slammed the door closed with equal intensity.

J.D. didn't raise his gaze from his work. "Hello, Mother."

"She had the audacity to offer to check my parachute at the door!"

"I should fire her immediately," he agreed with a nod.

Amanda hesitated. "That would be a little harsh, darling. After all, she's been working here since before you were born. What would the poor woman do with her time?"

J.D. tried not to grin. "I wish you'd stop dating that general, Mother. He's a bad influence."

"Isn't he, though?" she said happily. "But I can't, not yet. He's teaching me Jodies."

He glanced up. "Jodies?"

"Marching songs, dear. Some of them are quite racy." Her gray-green eyes twinkled. "Would you like to hear one?"

"Maybe later." He eyed his mother's dainty form without so much as a flinch. Amanda could look like the perfect society matron when she wished—blue-white hair expertly coifed, white gloves, the air of superior indifference. But looks were deceiving; he knew that from experience. At the moment, clad in a khaki jumpsuit and bright orange helmet, she looked like the Queen Mother during the Blitz. He raised one brow. "Skydiving?" he ventured blandly.

She nodded. "The General has absconded with a cargo carrier, or some such thing. I've been practicing my falls for weeks."

His stomach lurched, but he knew Amanda, though eccentric, was no fool. "Happy landings," he said.

"Thank you, dear." She stepped forward and sat gracefully in the chair facing his desk. "Actually, I didn't come here to tell you about this."

"I didn't think you had."

Her expression was serious. "I wanted an update on Rucker High School."

J.D. lounged back. His father might have underestimated her, but he had learned that beneath her scatter-brained image was a very determined woman, one who could still deal from the bottom of the deck, and he never pulled his punches with her. "It's a mess, and you know it."

"Yes, I do. But I also know we have at least two people on staff who could straighten it out with a little direction. That's why I sent you out there, dear. You have a marvelous way of cutting to the heart of matters."

One corner of his mouth lifted. "You didn't send

me, Mother. I outsneaked you with a surprise visit."
He had no doubts on that score, not any more.

She inclined her head regally. "If you say so. What
are we going to do about it?"

"I'm not sure yet." He should be, he told himself,
but Charly had done something to him. He hadn't
changed his mind about the project, but he felt the
need to help, if only to assuage his guilt over his
accusations to her. "I might check back on them in
six months or so."

"I see. And what—or should I say who?—is caus-
ing this uncharacteristic indecisiveness, dear?"

Her perception continued to astonish him. "No
one."

"A woman?"

"Mother . . ."

She nodded sagely. "You want to jump her bones."

The fleeting realization that Charly and Amanda
would get along perfectly made him squirm in his
chair. "That's a frightening thought," he muttered.

"What is, dear?"

"Nothing." He shook off his mood. He shouldn't
even think of changing his mind. "I'm going to rec-
ommend to the board that we forget Rucker, Mother."
He didn't want to admit how much that hurt.

"Why not just fund the project and supervise
closely?"

"Because we cannot give money to every stray dog
on the planet. They have to help themselves too. We
can't afford it now."

"I think you inherited too much responsibility too
early," she mused. "All of this dust has affected your
brain cells." She sighed and stood. "Sometimes you
sound exactly like your father, dear."

"Thank you."

"If only he hadn't chosen to tie up the money in
that silly trust."

"If only you hadn't given your diamond earrings to that poor little panhandler," he echoed.

She grinned. "Yes, I do seem to bring these things on myself, don't I? Well," she said, briskly pulling a pair of gloves from one of the multitude of pockets in her jumpsuit, "I suppose I'd better hustle myself down to the car before the General decides to do any reconnaissance. He bellows like a bull when he's thwarted, and I can't see Miss Pickles allowing him past her bastion." She waved happily and turned, but before she could touch the door, it was pushed open.

Miss Pickles stepped in, ignoring Amanda completely. "Mr. Smith? There is a *female* here who insists that you are expecting a *delivery*."

The disdainful way she stressed the two words made J.D. glance at Amanda in accusation. She shook her head. He rarely received anything unless brought by bonded couriers, and Miss Pickles would hardly react this way normally. But if his mother didn't arrange it . . .

"Accept it, and send her on her way, Miss Pickles."

"Yes, sir." She began to back through the door, but a small woman shoved past her before she could stop her. "Ma'am!" cried the secretary. She lunged for her but missed.

"Mr. Smith? These are for you!"

Startled, J.D. suddenly realized that for some reason he had expected Charly, and this slender young woman dressed in a shirt that proclaimed MARINA'S MESSAGES—WE GO ANYWHERE! wasn't her. The girl leapt forward and wrapped a handful of strings around his wrist.

"Have a nice day," she said with a grin, then spun on her heel and walked out.

Amanda gaped. "What in the world?"

J.D. stared upward in astonishment at the six

Mylar balloons bobbing with his every movement. A card was taped to one of them. "Miss Pickles?"

She flushed beet red. "Yes, sir?"

"Do something with these." He held out the strings, and as she took them, he peeled off the card. She bolted from the room in the wake of "Marina."

J.D. opened the card and stifled a groan, wondering what horrible crime he'd committed in his previous life to deserve this. "Since I didn't change your mind," it read, "why don't you make good on your lofty words? If you think you can do a better job, prove it!" It was signed simply, "Charly."

"Have you disgraced someone?" asked Amanda happily, unashamedly reading over his shoulder.

"No." His mouth tightened. Adrenaline surged through him as he thought about Charly's challenge. It was ironic, he thought, that he had been searching for a way to banish her ghostly presence from his life, and she had given him the perfect opportunity. He would battle her on her own field, by her rules, if necessary, and this time he would win. He would expose her faults, prove to himself that she would only aggravate not enhance his life. In doing so, he would help Rucker High School and rid himself of her memory.

It was time for a full-scale assault.

"What does this mean, dear?"

"I think," he said, "that the gauntlet has been thrown down, Mother." He smiled grimly and punched the intercom. "Miss Pickles, clear my calendar for the next two weeks."

The next day, J.D. stood against the same corner of the school where he'd first "run into" Charly, casually dressed in tan slacks and a short-sleeved shirt. Practice was in full swing, but he hardly noticed the burly team members. Just being this close to her again stirred something inside of him that he refused to give a name. This wasn't a pleasure visit. This was business, he told himself.

Her chestnut hair lifted in the breeze as she flitted from one knot of players to another, shouting encouragement and criticism with equal regularity. She was wearing a yellow T-shirt, which sported the slogan GIVE ME FOOTBALL OR GIVE ME DEATH! and he couldn't help but smile when he read it.

She turned and saw him before he could wipe the smile away. Her blue eyes widened in shock as she walked over to him. "What are you doing here?"

He raised one brow. "Didn't you issue an invitation?"

He had the distinct pleasure of seeing her nonplussed. "That's not what I meant," she murmured, then turned back to the team.

"What exactly did you mean?"

"Hey!" she shouted, stepping forward. "This isn't a contest!"

J.D. followed her gaze to the two players named Hogan and Esteban, who stood nose to nose. At her call they parted, but their tense postures spoke volumes. Trouble was brewing there, and his protective instincts went into overdrive. He drew closer to her.

Charly forced her concentration to the team. She knew J.D. was just behind her; she could almost feel the warmth of his body through her shirt. Worse yet, she felt comforted, as if a favorite security blanket enveloped her.

She frowned and walked forward. She had never depended on another for protection. She couldn't. If the team even suspected any weakness in her, they'd never listen to a word she said. His timing couldn't have been worse! Oh, why did she send him those stupid balloons!

"So what did you mean?" he repeated.

"I only meant for you to do some more of your famous paperwork."

"I might." He stepped toward her.

"Stay there. We'll talk about this after practice, okay?" Relieved when he made no other move, she shouted encouragement to the teens on the field. But after another ten minutes she knew it was time to quit. Tempers were beginning to run high, and she heeded her own inner warning system.

"Esteban! Shoot one over here!" As the football flew across the field to her left, she sidestepped but missed it. Damn, she thought. "Hogan! You!" His pass wobbled and wavered in the air and finally landed on the roof. Hogan was blocking material, not quarterback. And she could see by his mutinous expression that he knew it. "Okay, everybody in!"

When they gathered around her, she grinned at them, ignoring J.D. as much as possible. "Not bad, not bad. Tai, more leg on those receptions. We want to catch them, not chase them." A chuckle rumbled through the ranks. "Hogan, let's see what you can do with the blocking dummies tomorrow, okay? Knock the stuffing out of them!" His eyes narrowed on her, but she stared him down, her smile never wavering. When his gaze fell, she turned to another, then another, until the team laughed along with her, almost but not quite breaking the tension. She'd have her hands full this season.

Last but not least, she turned to Esteban. "All right, Mendez, coming along, coming along. You've got the arm. We just need to work on aim."

"Yeah, that's what Melissa says," Hogan said with a sneer.

Esteban lunged for Hogan, her proverbial trouble-maker. It all happened so fast, so close on the heels of her good-natured comments, Charly was unprepared.

Before she could do more than yell, "Hey!" J.D. made a dive for the combatants, separating them easily with more strength than she'd have credited him with. But she could hardly appreciate his prompt action. With an angry cry she waded into the group of teenagers and hauled him away. "Back off!" she yelled at him.

Surprise flickered across his face, then betrayal, then his expression went blank. Her heart twisted in her chest, but she resisted the urge to apologize. Spinning to the antagonists, she shoved them. "Both of you, cut it out!"

"I'll get you for that," Esteban spat out at Hogan, straining against her.

"Choose the place," Hogan replied.

"No!" Charly pushed. "Listen to me! This is my team, my turf. When you walk onto this field, your so-called code of honor is left in the street! Do you hear me? The wars are *over!*"

They glared at each other, then at her, and nodded. But she could feel the promise of retribution crackle between them, and she knew they wouldn't listen to her, not unless she did something drastic. Anger they had enough of at home. Her natural humor was the only weapon they seemed unable to counteract.

She let them go and crossed her arms over her chest. "There will be no revenge," she said with a lopsided smile. "Or I will personally take my own, is that clear?"

Neither moved, but she had their attention. They knew her reputation. "Furthermore, if you can't control yourselves, you'll both be off the team. Got it?"

As they swaggered to opposite sides of the pack, some of the team watched Charly with sudden, complete indifference. Mutiny was brewing. She hadn't won yet.

Seeing their looks, Charly forced a laugh. "Show's over for the day! All right you meatballs! Run it off, all of you! Five laps, then we're out of here! Hustle!"

Groans met her command, and few moved. She went cold, feeling her fragile hold begin to slip away, but she refused to budge an inch. "Okay, you win. Ten laps." Half of them began to shuffle away, Esteban at their head.

She impaled Hogan and the other half of the group with an icy stare, her grin frozen on her face. "Anyone for fifteen?"

After a tense hesitation they moved off, and she sighed inwardly. Another crisis averted, but no thanks to J.D.'s misdirected help.

Charly watched them until they were out of earshot, then turned to him, livid. "Nobody undermines my authority," she told him fiercely. "Nobody!"

His brow raised. "They were going to kill each other. I could see that a mile away."

"You never even gave me a chance to do my job!"

"I wasn't trying—"

"What are you doing here?" Her cheeks flushed with her struggle to contain her fury. "You don't belong here, J.D.!"

"Maybe I don't," he whispered, glancing out to the field.

Her chest tightened, because of the memories her confrontation evoked, or his soft words, she didn't know. The man infuriated her!

She glared at him. "Those two are the heads of what used to be the biggest gangs in town. I will not have everything start all over again!" To her horror her voice broke. She cleared her throat, fighting it, holding on to her anger. "It's taken me four years to earn their respect. Four years of hard work, and I will not let some well-intentioned"—she waved at him and groped for words—"whatever you are ruining it! Do you understand?"

"Perfectly." The word was clipped.

"Good." She whirled from him and searched the ground for the football, refusing to allow her emotions rein, especially in full view of the team. A strand of her hair plastered itself to her mouth and she spat it out, clearing her eyes to look near the building. The football lay where it had fallen after Esteban's pass. She kicked it, deriving pleasure by pretending it was a certain person's dark head.

That out of her system, she took a deep breath and squared her shoulders. Her flare of temper never lasted long, and she doubted the incident would do any permanent damage. There would be no fight, not with her threat hanging over their heads. Hogan was in the minority. She should cut him, but she understood his rebellion and would rather find a way to reach him.

Simple, she thought with a twist of her full lips. Just work past sixteen years of parental neglect and fix him like an old, forgotten toy, right?

"I wasn't trying to undermine your authority, Charly."

His soft words intruded into her thoughts. Her mouth relaxed. She just didn't know what to do with J.D. "Whatever you say," she muttered.

Silence stretched between them, broken only by the thunder of the team's steps as they jogged by on another lap. Charly glanced up long enough to ascertain that they were running companionably, then looked at her feet.

J.D. watched her, his emotions in a tangle. One minute she was cool and distant, the next sarcastic and acid-tongued, the next a hot-tempered spitfire. He didn't know which one confounded him more.

The woman had more layers than an onion. "I can't remember the last time I was chewed out so thoroughly," he said. "You're quite intimidating."

"Right. And you're the Pope."

Her words seemed to tumble from her mouth, and he felt a rush of exhilaration that her sense of humor had returned. He didn't want her angry at him, he wanted her to like him!

Hold on, he thought. This wasn't the way things were supposed to happen! *He* was supposed to keep *her* off balance, to find the breaks in her guard. Instead he'd found one in his own. No one had ever gotten under his skin the way she had. No one. And he'd had the best of them try.

"You're not wearing a suit," she said.

"No, I'm not wearing a suit."

Her incredible blue eyes twinkled impishly. "I had this horrible feeling you wore a tie everywhere," she confided.

"Of course not. I take it off in the shower."

"Good. Silk shrinks, doesn't it? I'd hate to see you strangle yourself."

"I think you'd love to see me strangled."

"Not at all! I've never held a grudge in my life."

"I'm glad." And he was, he realized. Then he shook himself, remembering his true reason for coming back. "Because I'd like to work *with* you instead of against you while I do my research." But he wanted to do more than simply follow her around here! To study her for an assault he needed to see her in her own environment. The thought appealed to him more and more.

"More research? You should loosen up, J.D. All work and no play makes you a dull boy."

That's it, Charly told herself. Keep it light. If he knew the intensity of her inner battle, she'd lose herself. If he knew how his presence made the sun shine a little brighter, the air feel sweeter, he'd laugh himself silly. And so should she for even thinking such idiotic things. She had to keep this on the surface level for her own sanity. She couldn't let anyone so deeply into her life that she couldn't get by on her own. She wouldn't do what her mother had done.

"So," she said with forced casualness, "what do you need from me? Statistics? Background? My thoughts on the degenerating educational system?"

"Yes, Charly, but I want something more than that too."

Something in his voice, some undercurrent of smug triumph, made her eye him warily. "You want the cafeteria menus for the next year?"

He chuckled, his green eyes warming with an emotion that lit up her hopes like a matchstick. "Uh-uh. You said it yourself. It's time I got out of my ivory tower."

Her mouth went dry. "What are you talking about?"

"I mean"—he took a deep breath—"that I'm all yours for the next two weeks."

Four

"You can't be," Charly said promptly. "My brother is coming to town next week."

"I don't mind."

She chuckled. "All right, I'll bite. What's the punch line?"

He sighed, his expression sober. "I'm not joking. I've decided to make good on my lofty words and see if I can straighten out some of your programs."

Her laughter died. She gaped at him. "You can't be serious!"

"I'm never anything but," he said dryly. "You said so yourself."

"I did, didn't I?" She mentally cursed her impulsiveness. She should never have sent those balloons. It had obviously pricked some latent guilt complex. But if there was the slightest chance that she could help the school, she would take it. "Just follow me around?" she asked. "See how the system works?"

For a moment he looked uncomfortable, but the feeling was gone so quickly, she thought she'd imagined it. "That's part of it, of course. But I want to get to know you better too."

Her heartbeat went into overdrive. "What do you mean?"

"If I'm going to find a solution, I have to understand exactly what you need. I have to crawl into someone's skin and be able to think in terms of the problem."

The thought of him and her skin together sent a shiver up her spine. But she was hardly the logical candidate! "David—"

He waved away her implication. "He's too set on his own way. And I can't exactly move in with a student. No one should know about this. I need someone who has day-to-day contact with the people, someone who has a vested interest in success." He shrugged. "You were the obvious choice since you'd issued the challenge."

He had a point, she realized. She had issued the challenge. But the thought of spending two weeks with him turned her knees to rubber. "What is this going to entail?"

He tensed, his gaze wandering over the far horizon. "Why don't we start with something easy? I thought your sense of fun was warped. You didn't, remember?"

"You want me to show you how to have fun?"

"Sure. Why not?"

Charly stared at him in disbelief for a moment, then she erupted into laughter. She had expected a lot of things, but this certainly wasn't one of them. "You're kidding!"

"I'm not," he said with great dignity. "I just want to experience the simple things in life. Is that a crime?"

She tried to picture him doing any one of the "simple things" that she did to blow off steam, and it tickled her so much, she burst into another round of giggles. He kept his face totally emotionless, but his shoulders were thrust back and his chin raised. He looked like a man who had just committed himself to a firing squad. "You don't know what you're getting yourself into," she said, still chuckling. "I don't think caviar and champagne are quite on my menu."

His brow furrowed. "Don't do me any favors, Charly. I want you to treat me just like anybody else."

He was really serious about this! Why would he want to be just one of the guys? Despite his supposed reasons, this whole thing struck her as out of character for him. But she could hardly turn him down now.

Her eyes narrowed as their kiss replayed itself in her mind. Did his interest run deeper than just in the school? Did he think something would happen between them?

He wanted the simple things, huh? Well, she'd give it to him, all right. She'd give it to him but good.

"Do you know what a draw play is, Mr. Smith?" she asked with a wicked grin.

"No."

She poked out a hand. "Then you've got yourself a deal."

J.D. had ample time to wonder if insanity was in his genes. It had seemed like a good idea at the time, but now, following behind Charly's battered yellow Mustang, he had had hours in which to berate himself. Fun, for heaven's sake. What had possessed him? And what in the heck had she meant by a draw play?

All he'd wanted to do was to find a way to set her at ease, to make her relax in his presence. And he knew she had some rather harsh preconceived notions about him. If he could show her that he wasn't so very different from her, she would trust him more, drop her guard.

Then again, maybe he was rationalizing. Maybe the true reason for his action was that *he* wanted to see that they weren't so different. Maybe he subconsciously wanted to find common ground.

His mind skittered away from that, and he focused on the bumper ahead of him as she slammed on her brakes at a stoplight. The woman drove like a maniac! She'd cleaned up the practice field quickly, too, without a word except to follow her. And he had. Into the worst part of town.

The houses around Rucker were ramshackle, but this neighborhood beat them hands down. The tiny structures looked as if the first strong wind could blow them away. If they had been painted once, the relentless sun had bleached them to a dull shade of gray. A mangy dog looked up from a pile of trash in which it had been rooting, and it lifted a lip in a halfhearted snarl at his car before going back to its task. J.D. saw no children, no autos anywhere, but a broken Big Wheel on the sidewalk indicated that someone lived there. Objectivity was hard to maintain in the face of such stark poverty. It was no wonder she was so defensive.

Charly pulled up to the curb fronting a shack. The porch sagged alarmingly, and it seemed as if it was the sturdiest part of the building. A sofa that was now no more than a pile of fabric and springs resided on its sloping floor. J.D. eyed it in dismay. This is where she lived? he thought.

"It's not much, but it's home," she called cheerfully as she exited her car.

Bracing himself, J.D. stepped out of his Mercedes, absently noticing that the street made Rucker's practice field look as smooth as glass. But he refused to voice his thoughts. She had her pride too. "It's"—he groped for an adjective—"cozy."

She roared with laughter. "You're a great liar, J.D."

He cleared his throat. "So," he said briskly, offering her his arm, "may I escort you in?"

"Oh, indubitably," she replied. Her hand settled into the crook of his elbow, and they walked slowly toward the house. "I *know* you'll like it. Nothing pretentious, you understand. Just the simple things."

J.D. stiffened. "Of course."

"Is it everything you expected?"

The excessive innocence in her voice made J.D.'s suspicion blossom. He smelled a rat and cursed himself for not seeing it before. She was kindred spirits with Amanda, he remembered.

It was time to give her some of her own medicine. "Oh, no," he said airily. "I expected something much bigger." He looked at her, then at the house, then back at her. He nodded, seemingly satisfied. "It suits you, though."

"It does?"

He had her, he thought with a chuckle. "The ambiance is perfect, that subtle something in the air." He sniffed. "Sewage treatment plant." His eyes narrowed on her. "Perfect for a load of garbage."

She halted and dropped his arm. "You're a stinker, Mr. Smith," she murmured.

"I won't make the obvious comment."

"Good. I'd hate to think I disturbed your objectivity."

"I thought you were straightforward," he said, stifling his disappointment.

"And I thought you weren't a stereotype. 'Simple things,' for heaven's sake!"

He turned toward her, feeling like an absolute heel. "Did I really sound that pompous?"

"You sure did."

"I'll bet you have a voodoo doll at home in the shape of a sacred cow."

A giggle burst forth, but she subdued it. "It's a stuffed shirt," she confided solemnly.

"I see." Something inside of him bubbled to life with her laughter. Confused, because this wasn't how he felt after one of Amanda's stunts, J.D. forced himself back to the subject at hand. "Who really lives here?"

"No one, not anymore. For the last couple of years David and some of the others have slowly but surely been finding more suitable housing for these people. The last family moved out two weeks ago, and we're razing it next month."

"I'm glad. I couldn't sleep tonight if I thought anyone was still living in these places." Before she could comment on his impulsive statement, he went on, "Did you say 'we'?"

She nodded. "I work with a construction crew during the summer sometimes. Where do you think my team gets its muscles?"

"You?"

"I don't sit around on my backside, J.D. I get involved. The only paperwork I have is destruction permits."

He sighed. "Are we even again?"

"Sure. For now."

Funny, he thought, but he liked the promise in her words. He'd never met a woman who challenged him so much. "Then can we start over?"

She searched his eyes. "You're really intent on this, aren't you?" When he nodded, she pursed her lips. "Why?"

He hesitated, then surprised himself with the truth. "I'm not sure anymore."

Charly caught her breath. His earlier comment and his honesty pleased her, but something in his green eyes tugged at her emotions. She saw a promise in the depths of his eyes, a promise of things to come.

Then he leaned his head down and brushed her mouth with his. Electricity shot through her; pure, unadulterated energy coursed between them. His firm lips caressed hers, evoking a sweet response that was echoed in his gaze. She felt warm, protected, and secure all at once. For a moment she gave herself up to the sensation. But only for a moment.

With a frown she pulled away and stepped back. She was confused. Sex had never scared her before, but this didn't feel like simple desire. She didn't like it. He was too appealing.

When she retreated, he sighed. "Look, Charly. I'm thirty-one years old and in fairly good health. There is no history of insanity in my family, so I'm relatively certain I'm not as crazy as you seem to think."

"I don't think you're crazy." She tilted up her chin. "I just don't like the idea that you're slumming."

"Is that what this is all about?" He laughed humorlessly, amazed at his own density. "I'm not slumming, Charly. I've been investigating these kinds of things for more years than I care to count, and your challenge just showed me that I've never taken the time to really get to know my subject." He ran his fingers through his hair. "Lord, that sounded pompous too."

"Yes, it did. But it was honest." She smiled. "All right, J.D. It was my challenge. I think we can manage something."

He smiled back. "Good."

"C'mon. I'll take you to my real house."

"Which is where?"

"Monterey. Mom left it to my brother and I when she died."

"Isn't that far from school?"

"I don't mind the drive. It's only an hour or so." She hesitated. "There's a hotel down the beach from me. You can stay there."

"I never had any intention of doing otherwise," he said softly.

Charly turned away, feeling foolish. "Sorry, J.D. I guess I'm a bit paranoid, that's all."

"Don't be. Not around me."

But she was, she thought as she started back to her car, and more confused than ever.

"Charly? What's a draw play?"

"Football, J.D.," she called as she crossed the dirt lawn. "The quarterback pretends to pass while he really hands off."

"Tricks."

"Misdirection."

"Wait, one last question."

She halted and glanced over her shoulder. He was frowning in real puzzlement. "What?"

"What's your last name?"

"I told you, it's this long and—"

"Mostly consonants. I know." Surprisingly, he grinned. "It's not Machiavelli, by any chance?"

Her mouth quirked upward, she turned, and crossed her arms over her chest. "No. It's Czerniowski."

He blinked. "Spell that."

She did, then pronounced it again slowly. "Cher-nyow-ski."

"Charly Czerniowski." He shook his head. "Good heavens."

"It's a real mouthful, huh?"

"You do this on purpose, don't you? Drop little bombs calculated for maximum shock value."

"It's a habit." She waved, indicating their cars, hiding her astonishment. J.D. had hit too close to the mark. What had she gotten herself into? "Let's go."

J.D. frowned all the way to Monterey, unable to shake his feeling that she'd reversed their positions. What had begun as a simple assault was quickly turning into something else. He was now the defender. The vulnerability he had glimpsed beneath her tough exterior wasn't as feigned as he wanted to believe. The woman was a complete mystery to him. Was that her appeal?

He shook his head. It was more than her mysteriousness, and that's what worried him. She ignited a fire in him, both in his loins and in his soul. She aroused his body and his emotions with equal ease. And he wasn't so certain that it was a bad idea anymore.

They pulled into a nice, middle-class neighborhood, and Charly maneuvered her car into a driveway leading to a little house right on the beach. He slid his Mercedes in behind her car and shut off the engine. The sudden silence was broken by the distant wash of waves, the shriek of seagulls, and the slam of Charly's car door.

"This is it," she called to him.

He exited his car. "It's not what I expected," he told her, and she grinned.

"You mean it's hardly a slum?"

"No, of course not!" He glanced over the neatly landscaped path, the two-story cottage painted a neat shade of tan. "It's just so . . . serene. I guess I expected an apartment or a condo or something a little less homey."

She shrugged. "I like it."

"So do I," he murmured, and followed her to the front door. A welcome mat sat on the concrete porch, which was bordered by tiny marigolds and some bushy shrubs. He could almost imagine a white picket fence and climbing roses.

She inserted the key, then stopped and turned. "It's kind of a mess," she warned him. "I'm not here very often, and I don't like housework."

"Neither do I," he said dryly.

She looked as if she was going to say something more, then she shrugged and opened the door. He followed her into the house and gasped when he saw the living room.

Dragons! Hundreds of dragons! Glass dragons, jade dragons, rearing dragons, roaring dragons, sea dragons, winged dragons. There was a little dragon string-puppet suspended in a glass case, a walnut room divider crowded with lead and pewter dragons. A cute green stuffed dragon solemnly regarded him from an armchair. A great bronze Chinese dragon undulated the entire length of one wall.

He had only a vague impression of there being earth-toned furniture in the room as he turned surprised eyes to Charly's grinning face. "It started as a joke," she told him. "I was born in the year of the dragon, and my brother thought it was hilarious. Then the team picked it up." She covered her mouth, amusement springing to her eyes. "I just realized! You were born in the year of the boar."

She pronounced it closer to "boor," and J.D. wondered if she'd done it purposely, but he had no time to ask. Without another word she walked to the nearby closet, opened it, and kicked her shoes inside. Out rolled a soccer ball, another shoe, a dumbbell, and a coat. She stared at the mess for a moment, then restuffed the closet and slammed the door. "Would you like some coffee?" she asked him calmly. "I always have a pot on."

"Sure."

While she went to get it, he studied the book

spines. Medieval history, sword-and-sorcery fiction, a huge book on . . . unicorns? Must have been from somebody who didn't know her.

She returned quickly, handed him a cup sporting a toothy critter and the saying STOP DRAGON YOUR BUTT, IT'S FRIDAY! and warmed her hands around her own, a cream-colored mug etched with a Buddha-like dragon. "Are you hungry?"

He shook his head and gulped the liquid. His eyes grew large.

"Hot?" she asked with a twinkle. "You have to sip coffee. Like this." She took a noisy sip.

"Thank you, Ms. Vanderbilt. But I prefer my creosote silent."

She laughed aloud. "I like it strong."

"Battery acid is smoother."

Her gaze dropped. "Look, J.D., I have to change out of my sweaty clothes and take a shower. Why don't you run over to the hotel and dump your stuff, then come back for your first lesson?"

"I'll stick around."

She peeped up at him. "Just be careful. My friends bite."

"So do I."

"You'll need to around here," she muttered, then left.

When she had gone, he poured his coffee down the sink and returned to the living room. There had been nothing of a come-on in her statement, nor any indication that she'd heard his own double entendre. It told him she felt comfortable around men, and he found himself fervently hoping it was because of her brother. But when he heard the shower begin, his body tightened with almost painful intensity.

He wanted her. He realized taking up Charly's challenge was no longer going to be as easy as he thought it would be. The very differences he'd hoped to use to expose their incompatibility now seemed to enhance, to challenge, to liven up his life in a way he'd never considered.

He was in trouble. And he didn't know how to counter.

He lay on the sofa, staring at the mercifully dragon-free ceiling, and forced his mind away from the erotic image of Charly soaping her naked body. She was turning him into a sex maniac! Baseball. Think baseball. Or the stock market. That was it! T-bills, compounded interest, the yen . . .

The emotional roller-coaster ride he'd been on over the past few days caught up with him.

When Charly came down twenty minutes later, dressed in jeans and a Hawaiian print shirt, the house was silent. Frowning, she wondered if he'd gone after all and was surprised by the stab of disappointment she felt. He might be dictatorial, but his request to see her side of life, no matter what had prompted it, had proved he was fair. She admired that in a person.

She entered the living room and heard the soft sounds of even breathing. Her eyes widened in astonishment, then she laughed. Sprawled on her sofa was the stuffy fencer, sound asleep.

A great feeling of tenderness washed over her. There was something about a sleeping man that always tugged at her maternal instincts. Maybe it was the tiny smile on his face, or maybe the way his lashes—longer than hers—swept his cheeks, or the guilelessness in repose, but she couldn't resist the impulse to brush an errant lock of hair from his forehead. He never stirred. She smiled, confident that he wouldn't see her sloppy sentimentality, and tucked another strand behind his ear.

She blinked, then choked on a spurt of laughter

at the sight she'd revealed. His longish hair concealed a flaw in the otherwise perfect Mr. Smith, she thought, restraining her hearty amusement with an effort.

Then she backed away, content with just knowing.

J.D. opened his eyes slowly, finally focusing on a huge, golden, *vicious* animal's head, rampaging across the wall. He flinched, felt himself fall backward, then landed with a thump on the floor.

"Li-Tsang is rather formidable," a low voice commiserated.

For a moment he couldn't remember why he was there, or why the voice was laughing instead of crooning words of love in his ears, as it had in his dream. Then he remembered. "And ugly too," he said, turning to Charly, who was curled up in a nearby armchair.

"No," she said, "just different. Different can be beautiful, and dragons show up in many cultures."

He heaved himself to his feet. "Do you name all of them?"

"Just the memorable ones."

A spark of pure amusement flashed in her blue eyes as she uncrossed her legs and stared up at him. "You're cute in your sleep. Like a little boy."

He took her hand and drew her to her feet, pressing her close. "I'm not a little boy," he murmured. "I think we both know that."

She drew in a sharp breath, her eyes darkening. He could feel her heart thumping against his chest and knew a moment of triumph. He leaned his head down, just the smallest bit, but she eluded him. Backing away with a little shake of her head, she smiled. "I think I've had enough of male egos for one day, thank you very much."

He frowned. Did she think she was some sort of conquest for him? Is that why she avoided the sexual energy that flowed between them? He had to know, to understand her. "Charly, I—"

"Are you ready to have fun or not?" she queried, her hands on her hips.

He restrained the impulse to tell her just what fun he'd like to have and instead said, "Lead the way, teach."

She crossed to her Fibber McGee closet, bracing herself beforehand for the tumble, then rummaged in it and drew out some plastic tubing and a roll of brightly colored fabric. "C'mon." She beckoned with her hand. "To the beach!"

He followed, mystified, as she walked north along the dunes, fascinated as her long hair snaked into her face. He wanted to bury his hands in that hair, tug her forward, drown in the taste of her mouth against his . . .

He cleared his throat. Lord, he hoped she didn't touch him again. "Where are we going?" he asked, working to keep up with her quick pace. She was in excellent physical condition.

"We need to get away from that line of houses."

They arrived at a satisfactory place, and Charly dropped to the sand, quickly connecting the tubing into a strange geometric shape. Then she carefully unrolled the printed cloth and deftly tied it to the tubing. A kite! he realized. With a picture of a rampant fire-breathing dragon!

"That's not a diamond shape," he commented.

"Of course not. Didn't you know dragons could fly too?" She grinned and held up a finger. "There's not much wind today, but I think you can do it."

She stood, brushed off her knees, and handed him the stick covered with rolled string.

He stared at it blankly. "You want me to fly a kite."

"I know," she said with a commiserating nod of her head. "I'm asking a lot, but . . ." She shrugged.

"Fly a kite, huh?" He glanced around.

"Don't tell me you've never done this."

"Of course I have! But not since I was about six."

"Tell you what. I'll keep a lookout for anyone in a three-piece suit. And if someone comes, you can wrap the string around my throat and pretend you're rescuing me from a dragon."

"You're laughing at me."

"Yes."

He tried not to smile, but it didn't work. "Okay, crazy lady, show me how it works."

It took them nearly an hour to achieve sustained flight, and J.D. felt the most amazing sense of accomplishment when the bright object finally fluttered overhead. "Good grief," he said. "This is fun!"

Charly reached up, touching his forehead with her palm and checking his pulse with a sober expression. "I don't think it's fatal."

He chuckled, then laughed aloud.

"Now let's see how long you can sustain it," she called from several feet away.

"Where are you going?"

"I'll be right back!"

"What if it falls! What if I break it?"

"Then you buy me a more expensive one!" came the faint reply.

Frustrated by her neat maneuver, J.D. jerked the string and the kite dipped. Unwilling to admit defeat, he fought it back into the air current again, and he realized he really did enjoy this new challenge. Charly and this kite had an awful lot in common, he thought. He had his hands full with both of them.

She was unlike anyone he'd ever known—fresh, open, honest. Charly played her tricks, but he had deserved it after his comments, and she *had* warned him. It was his own fault that he hadn't seen it coming.

The kite's movement and bright spectacle soothed him for the next few minutes, but the fun soon began to pall. Where was she? Had she simply abandoned him? What did he really want from her?

Mesmerized by the bob and sway of the kite, lost in his thoughts, he didn't hear her return. Gasping, he spun around to find her blue eyes dancing. "You pinched me!"

"I know," she drawled, totally unrepentant. "I'm afraid I have a thing for shapely male behinds. Comes from playing football, I think."

"I never played football," he mused, a wicked glint in his green eyes.

"Oh?" she asked innocently. "You like shapely male behinds too?"

"No, you—" The string tugged his hand and his attention snapped back to the wildly dipping kite.

"We're losing him, doctor," Charly said in a theatrical voice.

"Pressure's down," he agreed in the same tone. "The heartbeat is erratic."

"Save him, Bones!"

"I'm a doctor, not an aeronautical engineer!"

Charly shrieked in delight. "You're a Trekkie! I knew it! With those ears—" She cut herself off with a choke of amusement just as the kite flipped upside down and plummeted to earth.

J.D. felt the blood creep into his face. "How did you know?"

"I'm sorry, J.D." Her voice was anything but. "I peeked while you were asleep. They're great ears."

"They're pointed," he said in disgust.

Charly felt her heart turn over, and she couldn't laugh at him anymore. Deliberately, she moved in front of him, holding his defiant gaze. She reached up with her hand. He flinched back, but she ignored the movement and fluffed his hair away. "They're not really pointed," she whispered, her smile tender. "There's just kind of a curve with a hiccup in it."

His hand moved so fast, she didn't have time to react. It locked on her wrist and his green eyes burned with a fire that seemed to take all the oxygen out of the air. "You shouldn't have touched me," he murmured, his voice raw with hunger.

Then his mouth covered hers.

Five

Charly gasped, and the heat in his eyes sparked an inferno deep in her body. When his mouth took hers, the world spun madly, and a fire raged inside her, searing her senses. The scent of the ocean mingled with his sharp fragrance, dizzying her with its potency. He pressed her against him, and she felt a rightness she had never before experienced.

It was a gentle kiss, but with a groan he deepened it, demanding something from her very soul. But he wanted more than she could give, and she whimpered in protest.

He broke the kiss then, his gaze searching her face. "Are you afraid of me?" he whispered.

Dazed by his sudden change, frustrated by her own conflicting emotions, she answered more harshly than she'd intended. "Of course not! That's the stupidest question I've ever heard."

His green eyes softened, and he caressed the angle of her jaw with his fingertip, traced the curve of her kiss-swollen lip. "I'm glad," he said simply.

Her gut twisted with need, but she resisted her body's yearning. Desire she could handle, but not the demands, not this tenderness. Maternal love for her students was one thing. This soft emotion she could do without. She pulled away.

"You are afraid of me."

She shook her head, dropping her gaze. "J.D., you said you wanted to be treated like everyone else, like one of the guys. I don't jump into bed with just anybody."

"I never thought you did."

"We're completely different people."

"I know that too." He placed his finger beneath her chin and tilted her head up. "But maybe differences are what lend spice to life."

Her heart flip-flopped. His gaze was so intense, she felt it as though it physically caressed her. "And maybe you don't know how deep the differences run," she whispered.

"Maybe I don't care," he murmured. His lips covered hers again, and his tongue darted out to taste her mouth. His teeth nibbled, gently, teasingly, and she almost gave herself up to the sensation that crashed through her body. Almost.

Sensing her resistance, he drew back. "I'm not going to pretend I don't want you, Charly. I can't do that, not anymore."

She hesitated, but she couldn't give in to his power over her, no matter how much she wanted to. She grasped at anything that would push him away. "I won't be some other-side-of-the-tracks fling."

"Do you honestly think this"—he caressed her neck—"is the product of collective guilt?" He shook his head and pulled her into his arms. "I don't believe this," he murmured. "*You* are the one trying to talk *me* out of it."

She stiffened. Lord, it felt so good to be held by him. So good, but so frightening. "I'm a novelty for you, J.D. I don't think you really know what you want."

He drew back and frowned. "You don't have a very high opinion of my character, do you?"

Charly's mouth was set in a firm line. "You haven't given me enough time to formulate one."

His gaze locked with hers for long moments, then he withdrew his hand, raising one brow high. "Touché," he said with a ghost of a smile. "I think I have to work on my patience, as well as my humility."

"You'll get enough of that tonight." Her lips curved. "I made a phone call while you were flying the kite, to cancel some plans. We're going to dinner. At a pub."

The setting sun made a spectacular display of color as they dismantled the kite and walked back to her house, but the immediate plunge in temperature sent J.D. scrambling through her closet for a jacket for Charly. A flash of denim caught his eye, and he pulled it out, holding it in front of him for her to slip on. She smiled crookedly at his gentlemanly gesture, but slid her arms into the sleeves without a word. It occurred to J.D. that she had probably never experienced that sort of thing, and he felt a surge of tenderness for her. Pampering this unusual woman had definite appeal.

Then he noticed the back of the jacket. "Don't you think you take this a little far?" He ran his hand lightly over the intricate embroidery, admiring the feel as well as the sight of the green-and-gold, bejeweled dragon across her back. "Did you do the needlework yourself?"

She shook her head as she pulled her hair out of the collar. "My mom did it." She wrinkled her nose.

"Sewing rates right up there with housework and eating bark in my book."

He pulled a few stray strands from beneath the denim, brushing her neck as he did. She slanted a narrow-eyed look over her shoulder, and with an unrepentant grin he held his hands high. "Tell me about the place you're taking me to," he said, holding the door open for her. She hesitated, and her subtle uncertainty plucked at his heart. "Indulge me," he whispered.

"I'm not one of your society debs, you know."

"You're a lady, Charly. Allow me to treat you like one."

She opened her mouth, closed it, shrugged, and preceded him. "It's an Irish pub," she said as they walked into the dusk. "Not far from here."

"I wouldn't expect anything as mundane as an English pub from you."

She chuckled, and they strolled in silence until they reached a low building made from natural rock. "The man who built this," she said as they approached a wooden door, "apparently had one just like it in Ireland. He was too poor to have his brought over stone by stone as he wanted, so he made do with local material."

J.D. smiled, immediately charmed, as he opened the door for her. The lighting was what he would term intimate in half the room, brighter near one end of the bar where a group of people were watching a small television. The air held a pleasant mix of popcorn, ale, and an earthy smell he swore was peat.

Charly greeted several patrons, and though there were more than a few curious glances thrown at him, once she had made a general introduction no one bothered them at their little table.

They ordered burgers and beer, but before their

food arrived, Charly's gaze swerved to a massive shadow filling the doorway. "David!" she exclaimed in surprise, then turned to J.D. with an apologetic expression. "I called to cancel, but I guess he decided to come anyway."

"It's all right. Don't worry about it."

David waved, then moved to join them. J.D. felt something stir inside him when Charly welcomed David with a hug, but she treated him like a brother not a lover.

"You don't look any worse for wear after your ordeal, Mr. Smith."

"How can being locked in a room with Charly be an ordeal, Mr. Bakker?"

David looked startled, Charly glared at him, and J.D. regretted his impulsive words immediately. "I only meant that she's such a snappy conversationalist," he said.

Her eyes narrowed on him. "Uh-huh."

"Uh, Mr. Smith. If you have a minute, I'd like to tell you what I'm trying to do to amend the proposal . . ."

Charly sank her chin to her hand, listening to David's single-minded speech about his program. J.D. glanced at her once, his eyes filled with silent accusation, and she stiffened. He thought she'd set him up!

She turned away, trying not to feel hurt. This was David's idea, not hers. How dare he think she would push him after she'd promised her help!

J.D. didn't look her way again, but to her surprise, he didn't cut David off either. He sat, politely listening, as David droned on about the same things they'd probably both heard several times already. As much as she admired David and his cause, she wanted to convince J.D. herself.

It suddenly occurred to her that she didn't want David there any more than J.D. did. She wanted to uphold her end of the bargain and see what he came up with to help the school. At least, that's what she told herself.

"David," she said, cutting him off midsentence. "Don't you have something to do at home?"

His mouth parted in a smile. "No."

Persistence was something he'd taught her, and she knew he was an expert at it. When he showed no signs of leaving, she nodded. "Okay, David. Have it your way." She plopped her elbow onto the table and wriggled her fingers invitingly. "I'll arm-wrestle you for it."

J.D. hid his astonishment. What in the hell did she think she was doing?

But David didn't flinch. Eyes narrowed, he sat straight in his chair. "What are the stakes?"

"If I win, you go home and leave us alone."

David frowned skeptically. "And if I win?"

"Then you can join us."

Charly never lost her confidence, but J.D. threw her a long-suffering look. Even she was overestimating her abilities this time. Who did she think she was, Arnold Schwarzenegger? "Charly, I'll—"

She cut him off with an impatient wave of her hand.

"You won't kick me under the table?" David was wary, and J.D. suddenly realized he would be too.

"Of course not." Charly was offended.

"Or throw soda in my face?"

"Heavens, no."

"Well, you've done all those things before!"

"I won't touch you, I promise. Except for your hand."

Several people had gathered around as they talked, and J.D. heard whispered betting in their ranks. Glancing around, he realized that the patrons who had greeted Charly on her arrival were betting on her with obvious newcomers, who had chosen David. A wicked chuckle rose in his throat, because he realized that he would bet on her any day.

They locked hands. "Ready?" asked Charly. David adjusted their right-handed clasp and nodded grimly. "One, two, three, go!"

They both strained as their steepled arms trembled. David grimaced, and their hands began to descend onto Charly's side of the table. Then David's eyes lit with hope.

Charly lunged toward his fingers, mouth open and teeth bared. David gasped and flinched. Charly slammed his arm backward. Her friends cheered and laughed.

"Charly, you said—"

"I said I wouldn't touch you, David, and I didn't."

"You were going to bite me!"

"I never had any intention of that! I promised, didn't I? And I never break my promises."

He knew when he was defeated. "I just need to listen more carefully," he said.

"You say that every time. Drive carefully." She saw David hesitate, and she smiled. "Trust me," she told him firmly. "I wouldn't do anything to hurt the school."

David's expression softened. "I hope you know what you're doing."

Charly nodded, but she felt light-headed. She had just protected J.D. from David! Why?

Her thoughts awhirl, she tried to tell herself that it all came down to tactics, that J.D. could help the kids at Rucker more than David could right now. But she wasn't sure she was right.

When David had left, and the crowd had dispersed, J.D. eyed her in surprise. "You cheated," he whispered.

"I don't cheat!" She shifted uncomfortably. "I equalize. Look, J.D., I'm no fool, in spite of what you think. As much as I hate to admit it, I'm not as strong as some of these bulls. I learned a long time ago that sometimes it's better to outsmart them."

J.D. shook his head, totally confused. Just when he thought he'd had her figured out, she went all kooky on him. Nothing about her made any sense—not her background or her thinking or her rationale. "How did you end up at Rucker anyway? If your mother owned that house . . ."

She stared at him for a moment. "Do you play darts?" She began to rise. "They have—"

He caught her wrist. "I have to know."

Her mouth quirked, but she reseated herself. "You'd better be careful when you speak in that tone of voice, J.D. Someone with less patience than myself might be tempted to bust you one in the chops."

He refused to be insulted. "You want to convince me of our differences? Here's your opportunity."

Charly couldn't resist the challenge any more than he could. He knew that now. She smiled grimly and leaned forward over the table. "Okay, J.D. Here it is. My father was a gambler. Not the poker-playing kind, but the kind who dabbled in real estate and stocks. I think you know the type. My mother was his secretary. They married after a whirlwind romance, and Mom, being the fertile soul she was, had two kids. Dad couldn't handle the responsibility, and one day after he'd suffered huge business losses, he went for the proverbial pack of cigarettes and never came back."

J.D. carefully kept all emotion from his face. "What about Rucker?"

She leaned back, shrugging, obviously disconcerted by his lack of reaction. "We moved there when I was eight. It was a nice neighborhood then. You almost expected to see the Beaver playing with his friends on the sidewalk."

"What happened to it?"

"I don't really know. But by the time I went to Rucker, the wars had begun."

"And the house in Monterey?"

"It was a gift from my father during better times. My mother could never bring herself to sell it, but she couldn't live there anymore after—"

"You must have hated him," he said softly.

Her incredible eyes clouded over. "I did, once. But David was more of a father to me than my own. He helped me through my rage. And Mom loved Dad very much, in spite of it all. She was a true Wendy, and he was Peter Pan. He simply didn't want to grow up. You can't hate someone if you understand him."

"Maybe not," he murmured, thinking about his own family.

"Now," she said briskly. "With all that out of the way, do you think we can still be friends?"

He stared at her outstretched hand. There were a lot of gaps in her story, but he had two weeks to fill them in. He clasped her hand firmly and shook it. "Friends."

"Good. Now, about Rucker . . ."

While she launched into the stories of the team, J.D. listened absently. She was so hard on the outside, so brash, and yet there was an innocent quality about her that awakened all of his protective instincts.

But was it real or assumed? He didn't know anymore.

That night after they'd parted platonically, J.D. dreamed of a childhood tale, a story of a dragon who was only a dragon on the outside and a child inside.

The next day, after spending the morning working on his portable computer, taking care of bank business from afar, he went to football practice with Charly. He stood aside where the team couldn't see him. He was simply an observer. His revelations of the day before disturbed him, but his desire for Charly had begun to take on strong overtones, and he didn't know why.

After hours on the hot playing field, tempers ran high. But Charly handled them with strength and, usually, laughter. All went well until Hogan, who, she explained, didn't enjoy his new position, decided to provoke another confrontation. J.D. tensed as she bellowed into Hogan's face.

"No, Hogan, lower! Canines and felines go for the throat! You want to stop your opponent, not kill him!"

Hogan glared at her as he snapped his shoulder pads around, and Charly glared back. Why, she wondered, was there always one in every bunch? Hogan had great potential, but if he didn't start listening to her, he didn't stand a snowball's chance in hell of making the final cut.

He muttered under his breath and positioned himself again while the others in the blocking drill shifted uncomfortably.

J.D. stood in the shadows of the building, his body as tight as a bowstring. Only her comments about his ivory tower kept him in place. Every time one of the players got anywhere near Charly, he expected the worst. But she handled herself magnificently.

He frowned. He had come to do battle, and assault meant studying his opponent, finding strengths and weaknesses. But that was for purposes of defeat. He wasn't sure he wanted to defeat Charly after all. What was wrong with him? Attraction shouldn't become distraction!

His attention snapped back as she blew the whistle again, with more force than last time, and at Hogan again. His heart seemed to leap into his throat as she began to move, and he poised himself to jump if she needed his help.

"No!" With a snarl of frustration Charly stomped over and glared up at Hogan, setting her nose millimeters from his. "Listen to me, you mule! Low!" She punched him lightly, her fist hitting a gut like concrete. "Low!"

Hogan flushed, and though she wondered if she'd pushed it too far this time, she refused to give ground. After a moment of fighting with himself, he growled, "I'll do it how I want to."

"And you won't stop a flea." Though she knew she could threaten him with the cut, she didn't. Instead, she rocked back on her heels and smiled, a dangerous glint in her eyes. "You could always try," she mused.

"Uh-oh," someone muttered from the waiting line.

"I want you to do it again." She backed a few feet away, never taking her eyes from him as his expression filled with suspicion. "Only this time," she said, "I want you to go for me instead of the dummy."

"Huh?"

"You heard me, Hogan." She crouched in a defensive position. "You think your way is better? Prove it." She bared her teeth. "Hold me."

"You're not padded." -

"So?" Charly prayed that her dry mouth and pounding heart were apparent to no one but herself. "C-mon, Hogan. This is a chance of a lifetime. A legal hit."

J.D. began to move forward, panic filling him as he watched her inviting trouble. Hogan looked across the field as if checking to see if anyone was within rescuing distance. J.D. took another step. Was she crazy?

Then he saw the cocky grin Hogan shot his mates, his look of triumph, and the expressions on the faces in the group—especially on the one Charly had called Esteban. The teenager was rocking back on his heels, aiming a confident smile at Charly, awaiting Hogan's downfall!

Remembering the last time he'd interfered, J.D. faltered. If this was some ploy of hers, she would hardly appreciate his riding to her rescue, undermining her authority again. But the alternative was to watch her get smashed.

It was the hardest thing he'd ever done, but he waited, his mouth tight. If that kid hurt Charly, he'd tear him limb from limb.

Hogan lowered his hand to the ground. "Anytime you're ready, Dragon Lady."

She ignored the taunt and didn't break away from his gaze. "Call it, Tai!"

Tai called the play, and Hogan leapt for her—high. She ducked, avoiding his trunklike arms, and shoved her shoulder into his solar plexus, using her lower point of gravity to push him off balance and flat onto his back. She straightened slowly, briefly checking his stunned face for any sign of pain, and crossed her arms over her chest to hide the twinge she felt in her shoulder. "That, Mr. Hogan, is why you hit 'em low."

To her immense relief he gave a short bark of laughter and dragged himself to his feet with a reluctant look of respect. "I'll remember that."

"Good." She smiled. "Okay, everybody. Drill's over! Take four laps and hit the showers! Four! Not three and a half!"

When they were far enough away, she grimaced and rubbed her aching shoulder. That guy had a gut like steel, she thought. He'd be a great addition to the team, as long as the little attitude adjustment had worked.

"Don't you think that was the least bit reckless?"

Charly turned, gaping, as J.D. stepped from the shadows. Conflicting emotions warred in her, pleasure at seeing him and anger at his statement. Anger won, and her mouth set stubbornly. "He has to understand that I'm the coach, not him."

"He could have killed you."

There was subdued fury in his voice, and Charly bristled. "I can equalize with the best of 'em. And it's none of your business."

J.D. strode to her, grasping her arms. His heart almost hadn't survived the shock of seeing her go head-to-head with that muscle-bound kid. "It is my business when I see someone baiting a rabid dog, lady! This isn't a friendly arm-wrestling match!"

"What about your precious perspective?"

"What about your hide?"

"Don't tell me how to do my job!"

He dropped her arms abruptly, and she ran back to the playing field, blowing her whistle and calling the team together again. J.D. watched her, fighting his anger. Didn't she realize what could have happened?

He raked his hair with his hand and turned back to the building. Never had he met a woman who bounced his emotions around like a volleyball. She rattled his cool, and she prompted responses he had no intention of giving. No one, not one single person had ever done this to him before. His fear had not been objective panic over the welfare of another human being. It had been for her and her alone.

He was falling in love with her.

He swallowed heavily and stared at her as if she'd suddenly grown another head. He didn't *want* to fall in love with her! He wanted someone with whom he could share his life, not go head-to-head with on an everyday basis!

By the time the team had left the field, J.D. had contained his tumultuous emotions. Charly strolled up to him, her hands stuffed in her back pockets, her gaze steady. "Sorry for yelling like that," she told him stiffly. "I have a rotten temper."

"And I shouldn't have butted in."

She grinned. "We're even again."

"What about dinner tonight?" he heard himself ask.

"I have to get these playbooks squared away."

"Okay." J.D. couldn't decide whether he felt disappointed or relieved. "I have some work to do anyway."

"On your project?"

"No, I have a business to run." He frowned, wondering if she hung around only for the school's sake, but he really didn't want to know the answer. "I have a computer set up in my hotel."

"Really? You can have fun with a computer, too, you know. It's not just a piece of office equipment."

He turned to leave.

"Hey, J.D.! See you tomorrow?"

He nodded, then smiled. "Tomorrow."

The next day, Saturday, Charly treated him to a tour of Cannery Row. This historic district, immortalized by John Steinbeck, had changed drastically since his day. The old packing houses had been converted into shops and restaurants, and of course, the famous aquarium. The bright sunshine of the past days was absent as the sky clouded over in typical, erratic Monterey fashion, but it didn't seem to dim her enthusiasm. She reacted to every sight as if it were the first time she'd seen it.

They wandered the district with the masses,

window-shopping, which was the only kind of shopping she could afford there, she explained solemnly. She did, however, strain her budget by purchasing one item—a kite for J.D.

After a lunch of hot dogs and ice cream, Charly dragged him into a long, white building. Calliope music poured through the doors, and as they entered he saw why. "A carousel?" he asked doubtfully.

Charly shot him a silly look. "Carousel," she repeated firmly, pointing to the object in question. "Carousel horses." She indicated them too. "Ticket booth." She steered them firmly in that direction.

J.D. studied the carousel carefully while they waited for it to stop. It was a real one, a reconditioned antique. The motor had been updated and was housed in shiny metal faced with something that looked like a small calliope. Most of the horses were missing an ear or a chip off the tail, but the colors and the music made a mesmerizing combination. He glanced over at Charly. She watched with pure delight, a childlike smile of anticipation on her lips.

"You're going to love this," she said. The moment it stopped, she made a beeline for the white unicorn. As she climbed on she explained, "I like unicorns, too, but not as much as dragons. There's an old story I used to love. When Noah built the Ark, he just sent out a general invitation to all of the animals. They all lined up—giraffes, pigs, mice, all sorts. The last in line were the unicorns, the griffins, and the Pegasi. Somehow Noah had forgotten about them, and he hadn't built the Ark big enough. The last creature to board the Ark was the squirrel, who was just in front of the woolly mammoth."

J.D. chuckled as he mounted a dark horse missing an ear and one emerald eye. "What would Noah have done with a bunch of . . . Pegasi? Couldn't they have flown?"

"Practical to the end, huh?" She buckled the leather belt around her and sighed wistfully. "I always wished I could have been there to build another Ark."

"If they would have survived, where would we get the creatures of legend?"

She rolled her eyes. "You have no soul. Strap yourself in."

"I will not."

"It's the rule."

"I'm not six years old."

Her eyes narrowed on his mutinous expression. "If you don't, I'll—I'll sneak into your hotel room and cut your hair while you sleep."

"You wouldn't."

"Try me."

He buckled the strap. "This is silly."

"I think you need a big dose of silly, J.D. It's a surefire cure for pompousness."

He bristled at her remark, but as the carousel began to move, soothing him with its motion, he thought of his own parents, of his staid father and fun-loving mother. Had his mother ever tried to teach his father how to have fun, he wondered. If she had, it hadn't worked. His father had merely spent more time changing Amanda into the "perfect woman."

But perfect for whom? After her husband's death, Amanda had reverted to form, or so J.D. had thought at the time. Now he saw her actions in a different light. Why couldn't they have spent less time changing each other and more time finding similarities? Why had his father so stubbornly refused to try the things that Amanda had wanted? Though he'd obviously loved her enough to leave her his entire fortune, he'd always thought his father had looked upon Amanda as an oddity, an embarrassment at times, a liability. Or had he?

He glanced over at Charly. Wind stirred her hair;

tendrils floated behind her as their speed increased. She threw back her head, gave a cowboy yip, and swiveled toward him, laughing. At his intent stare, she nudged him with her foot.

"Loosen up, J.D.! Weren't you *ever* a kid?" Purposely, she yipped again before turning back into the wind.

He had begun this entire thing to study her in order to do battle. But he realized something very important, something he never really believed would happen.

He didn't have to fight her!

Exhilaration blossomed in his chest. Without understanding precisely why, he gave a great "Hee-yah!" and gave himself up to the feeling.

It was, Charly told him later, an historic moment.

Six

Over the next few days J.D. surprised Charly with the intensity with which he leapt into every activity she suggested. Gone was the staid executive who could wipe every emotion from his face at a moment's notice. Though he seemed strangely determined at times, J.D. never hesitated again. He played video games, fed the squirrels and pigeons at Lovers' Point, laughed over the sea otters' antics. He even flew his new kite with never a trace of the awkwardness he'd shown at first. Afternoons, he accompanied her to her coaching sessions, and not once did he try to interfere or lecture her. He even bought a pair of jeans.

She viewed his actions with suspicion at first because he still held himself curiously distant, but his mood seemed to hold, and little by little she began to relax around him.

One day they entered the school's parking lot to find Hogan standing in front of the main wall, drawing in charcoal. "Graffiti?" J.D. asked Charly as they met on the sidewalk.

She shook her head. "Get ready for the shock of your life," she whispered.

They walked closer, and J.D. realized that Hogan—the erstwhile bane of Charly's existence—was sketching a mural! What was even more astonishing was that the artwork was excellent.

Scenes from Rucker's turbulent history were spread before him. He saw the violence of a gang war, broken and bleeding bodies lying on the ground, the coming of David Bakker, baseball bat in hand as he faced the hostile student body. And in the last panel, teenagers and teachers alike were working to tear down the shacks he had seen.

"Hardly utopia," Charly said. "But we're trying."

Though color was absent, J.D. could feel the power behind the drawing. And it moved him more than words ever could. "It's incredible."

"It was something."

Her soft words startled him. He had almost forgotten that she had lived through some of those events. He turned to find the familiar hidden pain and wisdom shining clearly in her eyes, but now something overlaid it.

Pride.

His throat tight, he caressed her cheek with his fingertip. She turned to him, her brows raised. His mouth lowered to hers.

"Hey, Ms. C!"

She jerked back and spun away from him. "Hey, Hogan! This is fantastic!"

"Wonderful!"

Hogan shrugged at their praise and shifted on his feet. "I don't know if they'll let me do the blood, though."

"Sure they will," said Charly. "Blood and gore is this school's middle name. Now get into your gear. You have an offensive line to stop."

"Yes, ma'am, Dragon Lady, ma'am!" He gave her a mocking salute with his pencil and swaggered away.

"Everybody's a comedian," she muttered, then followed.

J.D. stood before the mural for a minute, then searched his memory for a name. When he came up with it, he smiled and made a mental note to call his friend at the San Francisco Art Institute from the pay phone. Hogan deserved a chance, all right.

The next day Charly arrived at practice slightly ahead of J.D. and nearly dropped her teeth when she found a well-dressed woman studying the mural from every angle. Hogan stood away from it and greeted her with scarcely concealed excitement.

"She's a dean at some fancy art college!" he whispered. "And she said this shows real potential!"

"Of course it does! It's one of the best things I've seen in years." Charly glanced at the woman, who strolled over to Hogan, gave him her card, and told him to call her when it was finished. "We just might have a scholarship with your name on it," she told him.

As her sleek Corvette pulled out of the parking lot, J.D.'s Mercedes slid to the curb. Hogan frowned at the car. "What's wrong?" Charly asked. "This is the opportunity of a lifetime!"

"I just—" He cleared his throat. "I never thought this would happen. I mean, I'm not into ethnic art or anything. Just stuff."

"Your stuff is your ticket, Hogan. Don't blow it because of some image you think you have to project, okay?"

"I'll think about it," he muttered, and walked off.

Charly sighed. Men could be so difficult sometimes. She jumped when she felt a touch on her shoulder and glanced behind to find J.D. "Did you hear that?" she asked in exasperation.

He nodded. "Don't worry. The door's open. That's all you can do."

He strode on ahead to the playing field, and Charly began to follow. Then she stopped, staring at his back.

He couldn't have heard everything! J. D. Smith had interfered again! she realized.

Charly's indignation warred with her common sense. But the fact that he hadn't blown his own horn weighed heavily in his favor. Eventually, gratitude overcame her anger. Yes, he had butted in again, but he had done it with no thought of accolades. In his usual, quiet way he had simply done it. This was the kind of paperwork she could appreciate. And he deserved better than her treatment of him over the last few days.

Later that afternoon she left J.D. on the beach studiously building sand castles, because she'd decided to let him in on an old family tradition. When she returned, he glanced up. "Everything okay?" he asked.

She nodded. "That's a great . . . castle?"

"Hey, this is a work of art!"

His exaggerated affront earned him a giggle from her.

His chin tilted up. "Observe the drawbridge, perfectly symmetrical, I might add, and the—"

As she dragged him, protesting, away from the battlements, she refused to give into the worst case of nervous jitters she'd ever had, mainly because she couldn't figure out why she was so nervous. It couldn't have anything to do with the fact that he hadn't tried to reignite that spark of sensuality between them. Of course not!

As they topped a rise in the sand she gestured downward.

"*Voilà,*" said Charly. "A picnic and a sunset."

J.D. shot her a curious look but said nothing as they walked to the plaid blanket and settled down.

Charly pulled out beer, apples, and ham sandwiches from the cooler and slid him a paper plate. "It's not Chardonnay and Brie, Mr. Smith, but it's food."

"I don't understand."

She bit into a piece of celery and held it in her teeth as she talked. "When I was little," she said as she scooped him up a monster portion of potato salad, "my mother used to bring my brother and me out to watch the sunset. We had to eat dinner, she said, so why not enjoy it."

"She sounds like a remarkable woman."

"Oh, that she was. She had the most amazing capacity for making even average things extraordinary."

He glanced at her quizzically as he opened his beer. "I thought you were going to treat me like everyone else. This seems too . . . special."

"Don't get any ideas. This is just one of the ways I relax, one of the simple things. Honestly."

He winced. "You're not going to let me forget that, are you?"

She eyed him askance. "Do you want me to?"

"Yes!"

Surprised at his vehemence, she chewed a mouthful of celery. He really meant it. "Okay, J.D. It's forgotten."

"Good."

His gaze roamed over her, and she didn't know whether to be upset or relieved. Quickly, she loaded up his plate. "Anyway, Mom used to do things like this all the time. She wrote notes for our lunch boxes—telling us she loved us, you know. She drew faces in the cinnamon sugar in our morning toast or made little animals out of marshmallows and raisins and toothpicks." She shrugged. "Little things."

"They sound like big things to me."

"Yeah." She began to fix her own plate. That was all part of her life before her father had left, before her mother had faded into a wraith who'd never had time for her children, only her misery. She hadn't spoken of it to anyone else in such a long time, and it felt good to do so now. "What about you? Didn't your mother ever do stuff like that?"

He shrugged. "My mother is hardly the norm."

"Oh, come on. There had to be something you remember."

His eyes grew distant for a moment. "There was one time. She took my sisters and me to the circus. I guess my father went along with it because it was something children did. But she took it one step further, as usual." He chuckled. "She managed to get us backstage afterward, to meet all the performers. I was ready to run away from home and become a clown. My father was furious."

She smiled. "The perfect profession. How old were you?"

"Six." He shook his head. "I haven't thought of that in years."

She shook herself mentally and finished her plate. "Sorry. I didn't mean to rattle on like that."

"Don't," he said softly. "Don't ever apologize for being yourself. You're an amazing woman, Charly Czerniowski."

Stunned, she stared at him. The intensity in his voice was reflected in his green eyes, and it warmed her in places she thought she'd forgotten about. She could get used to him, she realized suddenly. She could get used to his strength, his surprising laughter, and especially that look. It made her feel fragile, special, cherished.

She swallowed convulsively and dropped her gaze. "I'm surprised you can say the whole name with a straight face."

He didn't laugh in answer. "I haven't stopped wanting you," he whispered.

Her heart lunged against her chest. "You hide it well." Sarcasm tinged her voice.

"Would you rather I fling myself on top of you right now? Tore your clothes off in wild passion?"

She gulped, and her treacherous mind screamed, *Yes!* "Of course not, J.D. That's not what I meant." When she felt his touch on her hand, she jumped and held her breath, but he withdrew immediately.

"Who hurt you, Charly?" he asked gently.

She laughed mirthlessly. "Typical male reaction. A woman doesn't respond the way he wants, and he assumes it's because she's been scarred forever by another man."

He wasn't daunted by her forbidding tone. "Were you?"

She flung her head up, fury spitting from her eyes. "No. There are a few women in this world who are able to breathe without a man. Our hearts keep beating, our blood keeps pumping, our lives go on."

He smiled and leaned back, his face bright with astonishment. "Well, I'll be damned."

His answer disconcerted her, as it usually did. "What?" she asked.

"You've never been in love before, have you?"

She flushed. "So?"

He shook his head and tenderly reached over to brush a windblown strand of hair off her cheek. "So nothing."

His touch sent a shower of sensation over her skin, but she didn't pull back. Instead, her eyes narrowed. "Don't get your hormones in an uproar, buster. I am not a virgin, if that's what you're inferring."

"This has nothing to do with sex."

Her mouth firmed. "I'm not some kind of conquest."

He grinned. "I never said you were. Eat your potato salad."

"If I wanted us to become lovers, we could."

"I know that. Your beer's getting warm."

She struggled for something else to say. "You owe the bucket a dollar."

He reached for his wallet, plucked out a bill, and laid it between them with a raised brow. "Are you going to eat or talk?"

Charly was silent. J.D. Smith was either very sure of himself, or he really wanted to be just friends, she thought. Or was he playing some new game, one she didn't know the rules for?

She bit into her sandwich. "You have one hell of a nerve, Mr. Smith."

He looked thoughtful, then nodded solemnly. "So I've been told. By the way, I think you need to match my dollar."

She threw back her head and laughed.

Charly's laughter never failed to astonish J.D. It never sounded the same twice as she reacted to even the dumbest of his jokes. And he told lots of them over the course of an hour. Even after the sun had set in a brilliant pyrotechnic display, he continued to dredge up some of the worst punch lines he could remember.

"Stick to clowning," Charly told him. "Pantomime, that's the key."

Somehow the knowledge that Charly had never been in love had unleashed something within him, something he didn't quite understand. Over the last week he had explored the limits of his newfound realization about his parents and his prejudice. That's what it had been, he knew. A bias over a lifestyle that he had stubbornly avoided, simply on the basis of how unhappy his father had been. But he wasn't his father.

He thought of the women he had dated over the years. They all seemed like pale copies of an original. He'd been chasing shadows in the midst of colors he'd never seen. Like the sunset before them, Charly had a quality that couldn't be captured. She was the real thing. He loved her. And he'd be a fool to shut himself away from her.

But he couldn't rush her because he knew that there was more to consider than his own revelation. He was afraid. For the first time in his life he was scared to death that he would be rejected. Ever since he could remember, matchmaking mothers had set him up with their daughters, the Smith money a lure they couldn't resist. Charly wasn't impressed by any of it, and he knew that was the first thing that had attracted him to her. Charly didn't give a damn for any of the trappings of wealth.

She was her own person, and he was afraid that she was quite right. She didn't need him at all. Used to the demands of his kooky family, the responsibilities of his inherited business, J. D. Smith didn't know how to be useful to someone who didn't need a keeper. And he certainly didn't enjoy uselessness.

His assault had just taken yet another direction.

"Ready?"

J.D. glanced around the blanket, surprised that everything had been packed away. The chill air signaled to him that it was getting late. He stood and folded the plaid square meticulously. Charly shot him a look and shook it out before refolding it. "What's the matter with you?" she asked. "You kind of phased out there for a while."

"Nothing." He smiled. "What's the lineup for tonight? Movies? A drive down to Big Sur? Mud wrestling?"

She chuckled. "Sorry, nothing like that. Actually, I think I should turn in early. My brother's coming in tomorrow, and he's in a snit."

"What's wrong?"

Her eyes narrowed.

"Oh, come on, Charly, what am I going to do? Write it across the sky?"

"I guess not." She shrugged. "Aaron's in the army. He was supposed to be transferred here to Ft. Ord next month, but the idiot got into a shouting match with his commander and got himself a short tour of Korea instead."

"Not a court-martial?"

"It's probably what he deserves, but no. He's too smart for insubordination. Apparently, he had a company of his own this year—he's an officer—and it had something to do with one of his men. Aaron is ultimately responsible. He wouldn't tell me the whole story, which is typical." She winced. "The only problem is, his wife is pregnant."

J.D. frowned. "I still don't see the problem."

"A short tour is a year, *unaccompanied.*"

Leaving his wife to have the baby alone, J.D. realized. "Does she have any family?"

"Yes, but Aaron is devastated." She lifted the basket, which J.D. took out of her hands. It was a measure of her preoccupation that she made no protest. "Oh, well. It'll work out somehow. I invited her to stay here, but she refused. They're coming for a short visit."

Though he racked his brain, J.D. couldn't think of a single way to help this time, but he vowed not to give up as he led the way to her house.

A girl sat on Charly's doorstep, her shoulders hunched, mascara running down her face. "What in the world?" Charly exclaimed. "Melissa!" Charly strode past him.

"Who?" he asked, picking up his pace.

"One of my best students," she said over her shoulder. "Esteban's girlfriend!"

They reached the girl at the same time. Melissa's face lit with hope when she saw Charly, but suspicion clouded her expression when J.D. walked up behind her. "Who's that?" she asked.

"He's a friend of mine. Honey, what's wrong? How did you get here? Is someone hurt?"

"I took the bus. I—" Melissa opened her mouth and glanced again at J.D., but before he could leave, she burst into tears. "It's Daddy!" she wailed. "Ms. C., he's totally unreasonable with Esteban! I—I can't go back there."

Charly's arm circled her shoulder. "Honey, are you pregnant?"

"No." Melissa chuckled damply into her arm. "That would solve everything, wouldn't it?"

Charly faced her. "That never solves anything, Melissa. We've talked about that," she said sternly.

The girl's face fell. "I know, it's just—" She hiccuped and stared at J.D. again.

Without glancing at J.D., Charly pushed the door open and steered Melissa inside. "You go clean up your face, honey. I'm going to call your father."

"No!"

"Melissa. We both know he loves you. I'll lend you a shoulder to lean on. I'll offer you a refuge. But I will *not* provide a hiding place, understand?"

Melissa's lip trembled, but she nodded. "Can I stay for a while, though?"

"We'll talk, then I'll take you home, okay? I'll even come in with you to talk to your father. But ultimately, it's your battle." Charly's face softened. "Go wash up. I'll be right there."

Melissa trailed dejectedly down the hall, and Charly watched her for a moment. "Lord, I'm glad I'm not *sixteen* anymore."

"It sounds like Romeo and Juliet," J.D. whispered, his throat tight with emotion.

Charly slanted a curious look over her shoulder. "Or *West Side Story,* huh?"

"Charly, you were perfect with her."

She frowned. "I figured you'd be appalled."

His mouth lifted crookedly. "Don't sell me short. Or yourself." He trailed a finger down her face. "See you later. You have your work cut out for you."

He left her standing on the porch and walked away, determination lengthening his stride. He'd finally found a way to help *her,* personally, and he wouldn't let it pass.

J.D. turned off all lights but the low lamp beside the sofa, poured a glass of white wine, then shoved a couple of dragons aside on her end table to make room for it. He tuned her stereo away from the hard-rock station to an easy-listening one, wondering if she had any candles but dismissing them as overkill. When he was finished, he sat and waited.

Thank heavens Charly had left without locking her door, he thought, but he knew he would have gone in through a window if she hadn't. Some of the pieces of the puzzle were beginning to fit. It had probably been a long time since Charly had had someone to care for her. That, he realized, was the secret. Not sex, not even love, but good, old-fashioned caring. How long had she carried her burdens alone? How long had she played Atlas? The weight of the world could get pretty heavy sometimes, and though he was hardly an expert on relaxation, he would do anything in his power to lighten her load.

His dragon was due for some pampering.

It was nearly midnight when the door finally opened, bringing with it a curl of the mist that usually swirled in from the ocean after dark in the summer. Charly entered and gave a soft exclamation of surprise. "I thought you'd gone!"

Dark circles smudged her eyes, and she moved like an old woman. J.D.'s heart flipped in his chest. No matter how tough his little dragon tried to be, she gave more of herself to those kids than she cared to admit. Not even football practice had drained her the way Melissa's problems had. "I came back," he told her softly, rising to help her slip her jacket off.

"What's all this? Are you finally turning true to form with a seduction?"

"No, Charly." He hung up her jacket, kicking the soccer ball back into the closet absently before closing it. "If you'll notice, there's only one glass." He took her arm and drew her to the sofa, seating her with a small push.

"I don't get it. What's your angle?"

"No angle."

"I thought you said fencing wasn't sneaky."

"It's not. That's your game, not mine." He seated himself beside her, then turned her gently away, but not before he saw her puzzlement. "How's Melissa?"

"She'll be fine. What are you doing?"

He rubbed her tense neck gently, then used his thumbs to circle the base of her skull. "Helping you unwind a little, that's all."

"I hate elevator music," she murmured, her voice thick with fatigue.

Slowly pressing his chest against her back, he reached past her to hand her the wine. "Drink it," he commanded softly.

She sipped obediently, then stopped and spun to him, slopping a bit of wine over the edge of the glass. Her blue eyes flashed with sudden fury. "Hey, I don't take orders from—"

"Okay, if that's the way you want it." He curved his fingers around her neck and massaged. When he began to draw her to him, her eyes widened, and she turned back. He chuckled. "Chicken," he murmured.

"I'm not a chicken!" She tried to pull away, but he buried his fingers in her hair.

"If you make any sudden moves, you'll be bald."

"Rat," she whispered, but stopped her escape attempts. "I'm only doing this because of your violent tendencies."

"Of course," he crooned. "It has nothing to do with the fact that it feels so good." The tight muscles under his hands began to unwind, and he continued, talking to her in a soothing tone. "It would absolutely kill you to admit that I could do something for you, wouldn't it?"

"I'm doing this against my will," she muttered.

"I know that. I'm holding you captive." Her head rolled slightly to the side. "That's it, honey. Relax. You've had a long day."

His fingers moved to her shoulder blades, his thumbs to her spine. With gentle pressure he rubbed and massaged until her head drooped forward. His manhood surged against his jeans, and he swallowed heavily. His hand trembled. He flattened it, feeling the firm, sensuous curve of muscle beneath her shirt as he circled her back gently. Slowly he freed the material from the waistband of her jeans and slid his hands underneath. Her skin was like velvet. He stroked it, caressed it, his heart beating madly in his chest as he continued his self-imposed torture.

He encountered the strap of her bra, and with a quick twist of his wrist, it snapped open. She gasped and tensed, and he remembered his vow of patience. Reluctantly, before his hunger overpowered his rationality, J.D. withdrew his hands and stood. Charly turned bewildered eyes to him, eyes smoky with the same desire her body had lit within him. It was all he could do not to return to the couch and press her deep into the cushion, burying himself in her.

"Don't you just want to be friends?" she whispered.

He took her hand in his, kissed her fingertips slowly, and pressed her palm against his chest. Surprise lit her eyes as her splayed fingertips felt the wild rhythm of his heartbeat.

"Does that feel like the heart of a man who just wants to be friends?"

She jerked her hand back as if it had been burned.

He smiled. "Hide your head in the sand all you want, Charly, but we will be lovers."

And with that, he left.

She stared after him in shock. The rapid heartbeat against her fingertips had sent a violent stab of longing through her. And he had misinterpreted it! That noble, stubborn idiot had thought he could just soothe her, rob her of what little inhibition she had left, then leave her wanting more?

She felt anything but soothed, and her contrary streak demanded that she do nothing by his rules. It was time for the offense to take the field.

"We'll be lovers, all right," she promised. "And sooner than you think."

Seven

J.D. took a cold shower, and when that didn't work to his satisfaction, he took another. Afterward, nearly blue from the water, he poured himself a stiff drink from the sideboard and glared at the plush hotel room as if it were at fault. He irritably adjusted the towel slung low over his hips and flipped on the television. Nothing held his attention. Finally, in desperation, he shoved his glasses on and pulled out his notes for his own project with Rucker.

Thoughts swam between the words and him—Melissa's troubled home life, Hogan's macho reluctance, Esteban's pride. He shook his head. He was getting involved, more thoroughly than he'd imagined he could, and his approach just didn't seem to be enough anymore. David's original proposal made sense, he realized. To break the cycle, something on a bigger scale was needed.

He frowned. Charly had vowed to change his mind. Was this some underhanded plan of hers?

Irritably, he flung the papers onto the table, his glasses close behind. He leaned his head back and rubbed the bridge of his nose. How could he suspect her motives when she'd proven her honesty? Charly just didn't play those kind of games. Her face revealed everything—anger, pride, beauty . . . desire.

With a growl he tossed the towel aside, turned off the light, and climbed into the huge bed.

He shifted, but the bed felt too big, too empty. Moonlight illuminated every square inch of it with depressing clarity, and he considered shutting the blind, but didn't feel like climbing back in alone.

She was in his blood. His skin was fevered with the image of being pressed against Charly, even briefly. The woman would drive him insane until he could prove to her, and ultimately to himself, that she belonged in his life!

A knock at the door brought him bolt upright. It was probably some misdirected bellboy, he guessed. "Wrong room!" he shouted, but whoever it was knocked again, more firmly this time.

Grumbling, he threw his legs over the side of the bed and grabbed the towel. Wrapping it tightly around his hips, he strode to the door and grasped the knob, prepared to throw it open and curse in every language he could think of. But he decided against both actions. The person didn't deserve to be the target of his frustration. "You have the wrong room," he repeated firmly.

"Telegram for Mr. Smith," came a nasal voice.

Frowning, he immediately thought of his mother, of her skydiving, and snatched open the door. There, standing in the dim hall, was Charly, wrapped in a raincoat.

She shook her head and clicked her tongue. "The oldest trick in the book, and you fell for it. Sucker."

"What are you doing here?" His towel slipped, and he made a grab for it.

She chuckled. "Nice legs. May I come in?"

"I don't think—"

She ignored his warning and strode past him.

He sighed and closed the door. When he reached for the light, her soft protest stayed his hand, and he eyed her warily. "What's wrong?"

"Nothing. What could be wrong. I like this place. All this elegant blue stuff suits you."

"It's not a slum," he couldn't help saying.

Her rich laughter filled the room as she spun to him, her chestnut hair billowing around her. "Hardly."

"If nothing's wrong . . ." He trailed off, his overly active libido giving him one possible explanation. But he dismissed that quickly. "Is it raining?"

"Foggy, as usual." She pursed her mouth. "I just wanted to talk to you for a minute."

"Of course." He wiped all emotion from his face, but an inferno raged within. His towel was getting more and more revealing as his instinctive reaction pushed into it. "Would you like a drink?"

"No, thanks. I just wanted to say one thing, then I'll be on my way. Maybe."

He frowned, puzzled. "What?"

She bit her lip. "About your noble gesture tonight. You know, that 'leave 'em when they're vulnerable' mentality?"

He stiffened. The last thing he needed right now was another of her ego-deflating speeches. "Look, Charly—"

"I just wanted you to know one thing." She cleared her throat, holding his gaze as she undid the top button of her coat. "Nobility stinks."

He swallowed heavily as the next button she opened revealed the curve of a breast. "What?"

"I said"—she moved closer, continuing, inch by inch, to reveal more skin—"nobility stinks."

"You—" The remaining buttons were dismissed as she pushed the coat down her shoulders and let it drop to the floor. Glowing silver in the moonlight,

Charly stood tall and proud, her magnificent body completely naked.

A wave of desire nearly knocked him off his feet. He hissed a deep breath through his teeth, his hand clenched white on the towel. Mere feet separated them, but he could not move, entranced by the glorious sight before him. Bathed with light and shadow, her upthrust breasts were tight, the nipples hardened in the cool night air. Her hair tumbled over her shoulders, almost but not touching the peaks. The faint etching of the scar ran along her ribs, paralleling the indentation of her impossibly small waist. Her flat belly flared to rounded hips, and lower dark curls formed a V of shadow above legs that gently tapered into the pool of fabric at her feet.

As his gaze continued to boldly assess her, Charly felt a quiver run through her. Admiration burned in his smoldering green eyes, and his arms, pure muscle and sinew, tensed. A light dusting of hair covered his chest. He said nothing, but she could see his hand on the towel, holding it as if it were some lifeline.

He was beautiful, in that indefinable masculine way. His body, his face, seemed carved from smooth, hard wood. His eyes were alive with flames that licked her nakedness in an almost physical caress. Her hand trembled as he made no move toward her. Why didn't he *do* something? She'd made this first, all-important gesture, hadn't she? Was there something wrong with her?

This had seemed like a good idea at the time, but now, standing before him, she felt awkward, naked in more ways than one, and more than a little foolish. Maybe she had misinterpreted things again, jumping the gun because of a distorted sense of reality.

Her heart hammered in her chest, and she was

filled with a cowardly urge to bolt. "Say something," she whispered hoarsely.

His gaze snapped to hers. Untamed desire flared in his eyes, exposing his need more clearly than words ever could. She gasped, and every molecule of her being responded. He wanted her, all right, as much as she wanted him. But the awkwardness hadn't disappeared; if anything, it had intensified. Her legs had suddenly turned to water, and she couldn't seem to make them obey her command to walk to him.

"You're beautiful." His voice was raw, but still he didn't move. "Perfection as I'd never dreamed it."

She swallowed convulsively, amusement curving her mouth. "Corny, Mr. Smith."

He smiled his slow smile and stepped toward her. "A good dose of corny is the cure for armor plating."

"I see." Her breathing became shallow as he neared. "Dragon-slaying, Sir Knight?"

"No. It's too late for that."

His eyes never left hers as he reached out one hand. She tensed, expecting . . . she didn't know what. His finger trailed down her cheek, her neck, and farther. When he touched the curve of her breast, she sucked in her breath as sensation washed over her, but he didn't stop there. Gently, tantalizingly, his fingertip encountered the bud of her nipple and circled around it, over it, before moving to her ribs.

Charly's eyes fluttered closed, and she surprised herself with the tiny moan that rose in her throat. Never before had she felt helpless against her own desires. His gentle assault breached her defenses. A rush of dampness pooled at the juncture of her legs as his other hand joined the sensual journey, and her knees trembled. This time his palms caressed her face, his thumbs moved over the bridge of her nose, her eyelids, her mouth. He traced the delicate curve of her ears, the bold jut of her shoulder, then down her ribs to her waist. He caressed her hips, her buttocks, and gently pulled her to him.

His impatience had vanished with her shy request, but not his hunger. He fought that fiercely as he felt his stiffened manhood nestle against her belly, her full breasts press against his chest. He wouldn't let this go too far, he promised himself. He would just touch her, just worship her body, but he would resist his fulfillment as long as possible. If she wanted to stop, he would.

A tremor ran over her skin, and he knew he was right to go slowly. Though she had brashly declared she was experienced, had impulsively walked into his room naked, Charly had a vulnerability that spoke more strongly than her words. He didn't merely want her body. He wanted the part of her that was as yet unprobed. He wanted to assault her senses, to brand her soul with his, to show her tenderness as well as passion. And if that meant calling a halt to this madness, then so be it, he decided.

But not yet.

His mouth grazed hers lightly, his tongue ran over her lips, but he didn't linger there. He pressed a kiss to the firm corner of her mouth, trailed over her jaw to the erotic spot beneath her ear. Her whimper of pleasure almost undid all of his good intentions, but he ignored the fire in his gut.

"Touch me," he whispered.

Her hands crept up his back, tentatively stroking his skin. The hesitant exploration sent a shock wave through his body. His manhood throbbed between them, but he resisted its message. He had only begun.

He held her against him as he nibbled the chord of her neck. Sucking gently, he caressed her spine. She arched against him and her head tilted back. Accepting the invitation, he licked the skin at the base of her throat, then moved to her other ear and pulled the lobe into his mouth. Her nails lightly raked his back.

He groaned as heat spiraled through him. Pulling away, he cupped her face in his hands and rested his forehead against hers. "Noble or not," he said roughly, "I'll understand if you back out. If you want, I can stop this now."

Dazed, passion-filled blue eyes met his. "I can't," she whispered. Her hands tangled in his hair, and she pulled his mouth to hers. "I don't want to."

The bold thrust of her tongue drove all objections from his mind. He buried his fingers in her wild chestnut mane and gave in to the hunger he had kept at bay. He parried her, then explored the moist recesses of her mouth, not sipping at the heady flavor anymore but drinking deeply of her, demanding response.

She melted against him, her head spinning. When he broke the kiss, she moaned low in her throat, and he slipped his arm beneath her and lifted her as if she were a doll. Stunned, she opened her mouth to protest, but he hushed her most effectively, lingering over the kiss before laying her gently on the bed.

For long moments he gazed at her possessively, avariciously, devouring her with his eyes as he fought a nearly overpowering urge to bury himself in her immediately. Her athletic perfection went beyond even his wildest dreams. But he wanted more than mere possession, and that demanded a pace that he wasn't certain he would be able to maintain. Tasting her with nibbles and sips just wasn't enough.

"I'm cold," she murmured, her eyes wide as she returned his visual exploration. A shiver whispered down his spine, and he knew he wouldn't be able to go as slowly as he'd hoped. Not this time.

He stretched out beside her, but instead of resuming the kiss, he buried his face in her hair. Tremors rippled over her skin as his tongue circled the muscles of her neck. He ran his hand over her belly, stroking her, inflaming her to a pitch she never imagined existed. When she tried to turn into him, he firmly pressed her back.

"No." he groaned, sending a quiver through her. "Unless you want this over before it's begun."

And she couldn't find the strength to try again when his fingers swiftly found her firm breast. Sensation washed over her in wave after wave as he rolled the hardened nipple with his fingertips. But he didn't stop there. With a masculine growl he took it into his mouth and suckled deeply. His hand slid to the apex of her thighs, rubbing her with a flat palm.

She moaned as the moist heat of his mouth, the pressure of his hand, the tugging at her most secret depths, devastated her body. Some dim part of her mind heard his low voice, moaning words of encouragement against her breast, and they took her higher than she had ever been.

"That's it, love," he muttered. "Let it go."

A knot of heat wound inside of her, tighter and tighter until it exploded in a firestorm of ecstasy. She cried out in pleasure.

Slowly, while she drifted down, he withdrew his mouth and hand. He levered himself over her, his mouth brushing hers lightly, again and again, and she found that the heat hadn't vanished. His teasing kisses brought it back tenfold. His stiff manhood pressed against her, the rough hair of his chest inflamed her sensitized breasts. Sudden, overwhelming fire burned within her. A great emptiness opened inside, and she knew only one way to fill it, the only man who could. Holding him tightly, she took his mouth fiercely with hers and parted her thighs.

A single thrust brought him quickly into her hot depths, and he groaned her name as she arched against him. She welcomed him eagerly, wrapping her legs around him as she matched his pace, then, when that wasn't enough, she quickened it. She gave as much as she took, and when their voices caroled together in rapture, they were as one.

Their feverish movement slowed, their heaving, passion-slicked bodies calmed, their labored breathing evened, and Charly felt the most incredible sense of peace she had ever known. J.D. raised his head, and smiling tenderly, he kissed her. Gently, reverently, his mouth grazed hers again. His lips touched her cheek, her nose, then both eyelids.

"Hello," he murmured.

Serene, she smiled. "Hi," she whispered.

He brushed a strand of damp hair from her brow. "Welcome back."

Her smile wavered. She *had* been somewhere, a place she'd never been before. He'd taken her deep into herself, and somehow out again with his seductive endearments, his electric touch. The realization shocked her.

"Charly," he whispered, his gaze intense, "I—"

"Don't." She reached up to swiftly cover his mouth with her hand as surprise flared in his eyes. "Please don't say anything."

He pulled back, frowning. "What's wrong?"

"I just—" She blinked back sudden tears. "Nothing's wrong, J.D. Just don't go all corny on me again, okay?"

His expression softened. "All right. For now." He rolled off her and cradled her in his arms. "Don't be afraid of me, Charly. Or the way you feel."

"I'm not afraid," she whispered stubbornly into

his chest. Then, to say something, she added, "You're a wonderful lover. I'm glad I decided to come over."

He hesitated, but murmured, "So am I, beloved. So am I."

Charly lay in the warm circle of his arms as he slowly drifted into sleep. It felt so good, so right to be there, as if she had finally come home. With him she felt fragile, feminine, cherished. And that frightened her as nothing else ever had.

She eased out of his embrace and caught her breath as he stirred and muttered something, but he didn't awaken. She picked up her coat and eased into it, shivering as the cold lining touched her passion-heated skin, then slid her feet into her shoes. Tears filled her eyes as she gazed down at the man sprawled over the bed. "Coward," she whispered fiercely, but not to him.

Her hand reached out, but she closed it into a fist. With a deep breath she turned away.

No matter how he made her feel, she had to keep this on her terms. He threatened her existence. And she couldn't afford to get used to him. She was stronger than that.

She opened the door and slipped into the hall.

Something prodded J.D. awake, something terrible. The most precious thing on earth had been snatched from his grasp.

Then the evening replayed itself in his mind, and he sighed. It was only a dream. He smiled and reached out his hand. The bed was empty.

His eyes flew open and he scanned the room. Her coat was gone. "Charly?" he called softly, but heard nothing. He leapt from the bed to check the bathroom, but it, too, was empty.

Instinct took him to the window. The moisture hung heavy in the night, but the chill he felt had nothing to do with the fog. He glanced down toward the beach. At the edge of the water, shrouded in mist and moonlight, a tall figure stood staring out to sea. Alone, her shoulders thrown back defiantly, she tossed her head and let her glorious hair stream behind her.

J.D. touched the cool pane with his fingertips. "Stubborn, stubborn woman," he whispered. "What are you afraid of? Everyone has fears. Why won't you let me share yours?"

As if hearing his words, she turned and looked up at his window. He could almost see her face, the delicacy and the strength, the softness and the stubbornness, the humor and the sorrow.

"Come back," he murmured, willing her to return. "Let me hold you. Let me love you the way you deserve to be loved."

But she walked away, her form quickly swallowed by the swirling haze.

His heart twisted in his chest, his throat tightened, yet determination rose inside him. "Oh, love," he whispered. "I can't let you go. Not now." His mouth curved. "Just wait until tomorrow, Dragon Lady. You can't get rid of me that easily."

And with that vow, he returned to his lonely bed.

Eight

Charly shot upright, her chest heaving in the wake of the nightmare. The bright morning sunlight flooded her bedroom and she winced, shielding her eyes with her hand. With a groan she settled back against her pillows. She'd dreamed someone had taken a jackhammer to her head, probably J.D. after her callous desertion last night. She should have awakened him, told him she was leaving, *talked* to him. But she hadn't had the courage, hadn't even completely understood her reasons for hushing the words he'd almost spoken. Panic, confusion, and guilt plagued her and had kept her tossing and turning all night long.

The pounding came again, echoing through her skull. No imaginary foe, this, but a disgustingly early riser at her door. She began a colorful diatribe, but switched to less offensive words as she jerked her robe up from the cluttered rust carpet and slid into her battered slippers. If it was one of her students again, she would sear his or her ears with the inadvisability of awakening her at the crack of dawn, but she would do it without resorting to the cuss bucket.

She hastily belted her robe tight as she ran downstairs, then she flung open the door.

"Good morning," J.D. said brightly, and pushed past her, a paper bag in his arms. "I brought fresh strawberries, croissants, melon, and prosciutto."

She gaped at him as he strode into her kitchen. Numbly, she followed, wondering if he was insane or simply masochistic to awaken her so early.

Then again, she silently admitted, maybe he understood her better than she did herself, because a part of her was turning somersaults with joy. As she entered the kitchen he was emptying the contents of the bag onto the counter. The wind had blown his dark hair so that the tilted tips of his ears showed clearly, and she resisted the most incredible urge to run her tongue into those little dips, as she had last night. His fine features, his muscular frame beneath the casual shirt and jeans, all had imprinted themselves firmly on her senses. The memory of their loving left her itching to touch him.

But she couldn't. With firm resolve she banished those memories to the deep recesses of her mind where they belonged.

"I'm going to make the coffee this time," he told her firmly, holding up a tiny container. "German. Since you like it like mud, you might as well drink good mud."

"J.D.—"

"The croissants are still warm." He broke off a piece and stuffed it in her mouth.

The flaky pastry melted on her tongue. "J.D.," she began again.

"Don't talk with your mouth full."

She swallowed. "I don't eat break—"

He followed the roll with a strawberry, cutting her off. While her jaws worked to chew the huge berry, he grinned and began to slice the cantaloupe. "I'll have to remember this. If I ever want you quiet again, I'll just feed you."

Juice dribbled down her chin, and she snatched a paper towel to catch the trickle. Frustrated, she spoke anyway, her voice muffled. "Wha' are you doin' here?"

"I had to find out if you'd respect me in the morning," he said blandly.

She shivered in apprehension. She did respect him. That was the problem. "About last ni'—"

He held up a piece of melon in a threatening manner, and she stopped the words with a gulp.

He gave her a smug smile. "That's better. Is your brother due in this morning?" She shook her head. "This afternoon?" She nodded. "Then you have time to eat." He took her by the shoulders. "Now, why don't you run upstairs and change into something a little less"—his darkened gaze raked over her, and her skin tingled—"a little less alluring."

She started to laugh. "You've been cloistered too long."

"Sir Galahad was in the cloister," he murmured, his voice husky. "You've got your knights mixed up. Lord, how could anyone look so sexy in a fuzzy robe and slippers . . . that wild tangle of hair . . ."

Her breath caught as his head lowered to hers. She paced backward, her eyes wide.

His intensity changed to an exaggerated leer. "Frightened, little girl?"

She shook her head. "I haven't brushed my teeth yet."

"Dragon breath?" he asked solemnly.

"Buzzard killing," she agreed with a nod.

"I'll risk it," he whispered, and kissed her softly on the mouth. "Good morning, beloved."

She gulped. "Morning."

He frowned and leaned down. His tongue trailed the length of her jaw. Her heartbeat went into overdrive.

"Missed some juice," he said as he raised his head. "I think they're a bit overripe."

"I—" Her mouth worked but she couldn't seem to speak. "You— "

"And after breakfast you can teach me to play the game you've taught so well for so long."

She blanched. "J.D., I—"

"Football," he said firmly, and was rewarded with a startled laugh.

"Football?" She giggled, relief washing over her.

"Football. You know, pigskins? Rushing?"

"Tight ends?"

"That's the one. Now"—he kissed her again, hoping to keep her off balance before her mind could kick in with doubts again—"go brush your teeth." When she didn't move, he turned her by the shoulders and playfully swatted her bottom. "Go."

Charly took two steps, then stopped and glanced back, prepared to protest. He brandished a croissant, his brow raised in silent challenge. Bemused, she decided not to test his resolve and left the room.

Later, dressed in a Stanford jersy and jeans, Charly refused his breakfast and drank only the excellent coffee. She matched his light mood, determined not to show how much he'd disturbed her peace of mind. She wrinkled her nose. "How can you eat at this ungodly hour?"

He shrugged. "I guess I worked up an appetite last night."

The reminder hit home, and she neatly sidestepped it by lowering her eyes.

When he was finished, she grabbed a football and led the way to the beach. They tossed it between them for a while, Charly gauging his arm, which was excellent. With J.D. once again acting like an unthreatening friend, she began to relax.

"Okay," she called finally. "Let's see how you do

with a moving target." She walked to him. "I'll be the center as well as the receiver. After I snap the ball, I'll run out, and you pass it to me, okay?"

"Got it."

She paused. "Are you going to be here on Labor Day?"

"I'd planned on it. Why?"

She shrugged, seemingly casual. "I usually have a party to celebrate the new team, and the beginning of school."

He smiled, and her insides turned to mush. "I'll be there."

"Good." That wasn't what she meant to say at all, but his gaze washed over her like the warm tickle of summer grass, and she couldn't think rationally. She blinked and forced a chuckle. "Then this is a matter of survival."

"What do you mean?"

"Impromptu games have a tendency to break out like a rash." She peeped up at him, picturing him head-to-head with the bulls on the team. "You may not think this is so much fun after a while."

"I'll tell you when I've had enough."

She shrugged and realized this had suddenly become important to her. But she didn't know why.

After briefly explaining the play, she placed the ball in the sand, bent into position, and waited. "J.D.? You're supposed to call."

"Call?"

His voice sounded so peculiar that she sneaked a look back under her arm. His eyes were glazed. "What's wrong?"

He cleared his throat. "I'm not sure I can do this," he said.

"Don't be nervous, you'll do fine."

"I'm not nervous," he said faintly. "I'm . . . distracted. Don't you have any jeans that don't fit quite so tightly?"

Charly straightened, hands on hips, and swiveled her upper body toward him. "Just keep your eye on the ball, Mr. Quarterback."

"I'll try, Ms. Center, but it won't be easy."

His teasing tone shoved all of her uncertainties aside. Bantering she could handle, even with sexual overtones. In fact, she silently admitted, a little spice added interest. "Look at it this way. When we make a good play, we get to pat each other's bottom."

He leered. "I knew I'd find some reason to like this game."

She chuckled and repositioned herself.

"Set. Hut, hut!"

Charly tossed the ball between her legs. It dropped to the sand. "Uh—J.D.? You're supposed to keep your eye on the ball—and your hands in position."

He patted the object under his hands. "I happen to like the position my hands are in."

"You know what happens to quarterbacks who can't catch a football?"

"Um . . ."

"The centers start aiming a little higher."

"Gotcha." He grinned. "Let's try again."

This time he kept his hands off his center's strained seam, but threw the ball over her head. The next time he grounded it. But the third time it sailed lightly through the air to nestle in her arms. She ran over an imaginary goal line and spiked the ball into the sand, doing a little touchdown dance. As she tripped back to reposition for another try, his eager hand patted her bottom firmly.

"Definitely a fun game," he muttered, his eyes twinkling. "Care to score again?"

"Are we speaking of field time?" He slid his arms around her waist, pulling her to him. "I didn't think so," she murmured against his mouth. After a breathless moment she pulled back. "It's a great motivation to succeed, Mr. Quarterback."

"You're a slave driver," he said with a groan, but went back to practice. Whether it was the incentive or true talent, Charly didn't know, but J.D. became very good with short passes. His distance throws were wobbly, but she saw definite progress.

"Now for defense," she commented briskly, wiping perspiration from her brow.

Panting, J.D. toppled backward into the sand. "She's trying to kill me," he told the seagulls.

While she showed him the moves he'd watched her teach the team all week, Charly threw in little bits about the intramural games she'd organized, the first step she had taken after the gang wars had stopped. They rotated players in those games, so from quarter to quarter the same two people were never against each other. She'd begun that, she explained, because the first year one of the players had nearly broken another's neck.

"In spite of David's excellent programs, their mentality was set in many ways. Still is, for that matter, though not as obviously. But my semester was shaky, mostly due to the gang that Hogan heads now. Their turf was up for grabs, and by the third quarter he'd figured out the other guy's weakness. He taunted him into making a mistake. I can't afford to let that happen again."

"Don't they talk to each other?" he asked. "Swap information?"

"Sure. But when you're going head-to-head with the same person for over an hour, tension runs higher than if the scenery changes once in a while."

"What about you? You're a teacher. Aren't you a target at your parties?"

"Oh, I have a few tricks up my sleeve. Equalize, always equalize."

"I think I see a reason behind your insults," he murmured.

She blinked, then her eyes took on a wicked glint. "I think you're ready for the real thing. You're offense. Just try and get past me."

He ran straight toward her, and she didn't move. J.D. frowned a bit—he'd seen her grin in that same taunting way at Hogan—but continued. Just before he was within arm's reach she dove to the sand and rolled. J.D. was downed like a ninepin. There was a moment of startled silence, then both burst into laughter.

"One of your tricks?"

"You ain't seen nothin' yet!"

After half an hour, most of which she spent watching J.D. pick sand out of his teeth, Charly got the ball. J.D. grabbed her, but had learned his lesson in trying to bring her down the normal way. She equalized him to pieces. He dug his fingers into her rib cage. She shrieked with laughter and dropped the ball. His tormenting hands slid around her rib cage to settle in the small of her back, gently forcing her unresisting body toward him.

"You're learning," she whispered against his mouth.

Sinking into the sand, he murmured, "I think so too."

He kissed her with the possessive passion he'd locked inside himself all day, delving deeply into the moist recesses of her mouth. She tasted like coffee, smelled like soap, and was the most exciting woman he'd ever met. Beneath him, her vibrant body tensed, and she withdrew, breathless but with resolution in her eyes.

"You have to be careful with things like this," she said. "I have a friend from back east who moved to L.A. He and a lady friend were . . . engaged one moonlit night on the beach. At the crucial moment they were suddenly surrounded by people with flashlights and buckets." She chuckled. "The grunion were running."

"There're no grunion here." He lowered his head, but she evaded him.

"My turn," she said, and wriggled out.

He sighed, but stood.

"I'll call," she said. "Then you run out, count to five, and turn."

"All right, all right." He positioned the ball, bent, and waited for her call. And waited. He glanced back, amused to see her staring at his backside. "Charly?"

"I think I see your point," she said.

"This is the most important part!" she told him near the end of their session.

"I won't."

"J.D., honestly! You have to learn this."

"I thought it was illegal in pro ball."

"This isn't pro ball."

He sighed. "Why can't I just say 'Yeah'?"

"The touchdown dance is integral to the game! Now, let's try it again. Flap your legs . . ."

The sun was well over its apex when they finally called a halt to the game. She peeled her damp jersy away from her skin. "I'm sticky. And I have enough sand in my hair to make another beach."

"Me too." He leaned over and ruffled his walnut locks, watching in some amusement as sand flew into the air. "I could use a shower before we go."

She froze. "Go where?"

He glanced up. "To pick up your brother from the airport."

"I don't want you to go!" She blinked and turned away. "I mean, thanks for the offer, but . . ."

"You don't want me to meet your brother?"

"J.D., he has a lot on his mind right now with

Julia pregnant and his orders a mess. I just don't want to add to it."

"How would I add to it?" He took her shoulders and turned her to him. "Are you ashamed of me?"

"Of course not." She giggled. "That would be a real role reversal, wouldn't it?"

He grinned. She didn't believe any of that garbage about their backgrounds any more than he did. But his smile faded. "Then why don't you want me to go along?"

She groped for words. "Aaron's violent. If he found out you'd disgraced his sister, he'd have your head."

"Is that supposed to scare me off? C'mon, you can do better than that."

Her gaze locked with his. "I don't know," she said finally. "I guess—I guess your meeting my family would feel too . . . close."

"Because I'd find out the deep, dark truth about you?"

"Don't read any deep meaning into this, okay? I don't want you to come because I'm not sure"—her gaze dropped—"I'm not sure how I feel right now. I don't want you in my life, J.D.!"

He let the silence stretch. "Okay, what about dinner later?"

"Stop it. Don't make me laugh, it won't work." She pulled out of his hands. "I'm going to take Aaron and Julia somewhere. A *family* dinner."

Frustrated, J.D. could find no way to counteract her withdrawl, not without aggravating the contrary streak he was determined to erode. He left her at her house and returned to his hotel. He had watched her walk away last night, and though there was no fog this time, he felt her defenses closing around her as thoroughly as the mist had. Somehow she had won this round, and he'd never seen the feint.

She was confused, he thought as he showered, yet

somehow he knew without a doubt that if he stormed their family dinner, she'd walk away forever. But if he didn't do something soon, he would lose her anyway!

Someone pounded on the door as he wrapped his towel tightly around his hips, and his spirits soared. "Charly?" he cried as he opened the door.

"Goodness, dear. Do you greet everyone like that? It's no wonder you always get better service than I do."

He stiffened and leaned against the doorjamb, a mild scowl darkening his features. "What are you doing here, Mother?" And in her society-matron armor, he thought with a wince.

She gasped, and one neatly gloved hand covered her coral-painted mouth, though amusement sparkled in her eyes. "Heavens! Have I interrupted something, dear?" she asked as she scanned his room. "Is your lady friend here? Should I disappear?"

He sighed. He could never stay angry at her, though he had tried for thirty-one years. With an exaggerated bow and a tilt of his full lips, he ushered her in. "Empty, Mother. Or would you care to examine the dust beneath the bed?"

She entered. "Thank you, but no, dear. I can't stay long, but I was in the area . . ."

"So you decided to nose around."

"Of course! What are mothers for?"

J.D. gathered up his jeans and shirt, then changed quickly in the bathroom. It was never a good idea to leave Amanda alone in one's room too long, he knew. When he returned, she was eyeing a large, brightly colored object in disbelief.

"It's a kite, Mother," he said with a faint grin.

"I know what it is, dear. I'm just shocked to find it here."

He took it from her and seated himself in one of

the armchairs, stretching his long legs out before him. "How did you *happen* to be in the area?" he asked with a trace of sarcasm.

"It's a fund-raiser, Mrs. Barrington-Smythe's." She lifted her nose and raised a lorgnette to her eyes from the chain around her neck, suddenly the picture of haughty nobility. "Of the Pacific Grove Smythes. You know how she is, darling. It's that *y* and *e* in her name. It has damaged her already overblown head. I'm meeting the General for din—" She blinked and let the glasses fall. "Good heavens, are those blue jeans?"

"Yes. Is there anything else?"

Amanda seemed to be struggling for composure and couldn't take her eyes from her son's attire. "Yes, I—you haven't checked your messages in quite some time. The board is fuming at your absence, and I didn't know what to tell them." She sank into the opposite chair, shaking her head. "Blue jeans." She brightened. "Would this have anything to do with the balloon lady?"

"Her name is Charly Czerniowski, Mother, as you well know."

"Do I?"

A tiny doubt intruded into his mind, but he shoved it away. "I'm going to marry her."

"She wants to trade something as wonderful as that name for something as mundane as Smith? When's the wedding, dear?"

"As soon as I can drag her away from her football field."

Her eyes twinkled. "And of course, she has nothing to say about it."

"Not if I can help it."

Her smile faded at the serious determination in his voice. "I thought for a moment that you might be kidding, dear. But I forgot how much of your father you have in you." She sighed. "He swept me off my feet too."

"I'm not sweeping anybody off her feet. In fact, I'm trying very hard to give her some time to sort out her feelings."

She shook her head. "You're a bulldozer, dear. You always have been."

J.D. wondered if he'd pushed Charly too hard, if that was the reason behind her withdrawal. Then he wondered if he'd pushed hard enough. "Mother? If he hadn't swept you off your feet, would you have married him anyway?"

Their gazes locked for several moments, then Amanda dropped hers to the floor. "I don't know." She sighed again and turned away. "I was a sad trial to that man, J.D. I loved him with all my heart and soul, and I did my best to be what he wanted me to be. But he wasn't willing to do the same for me, and I became more and more rebellious." She shook her head. "Maybe if I'd known that ahead of time, it would have saved us a lot of pain."

"It was a different age, Mother. Women were expected to change, to adapt to their husbands." He reached over to clasp her hand, and she glanced up with misty, startled eyes. "I understand a lot more than I did a week ago, you know. I won't ask that of Charly, or even myself. I'm discovering I'm more your son than I thought, and I'm not going to sit in judgment of you or father."

"Thank you, dear. I know that. I also know that you think I'm a bit of an odd duck, but you know what? I'm happy with my life. I like myself."

His throat tightened. "I like you, too, Mother. Duck and all."

She squeezed his hand and dropped it, her expression turning wistful. "I just wish I could have seen what he wanted for me." She sniffed. "But in those days, living in sin was hardly the norm."

J.D. considered asking Charly to live with him, but discarded the idea almost immediately. Her departure the night before suggested a distinct fear of just the kind of day-to-day intimacy that living together would entail. Each time he had helped someone, she had pulled back, as if a necessary support had been nibbled away. Her students, her brother, her lifestyle, everything had been excuses to escape him. She held up her world—and everyone in it—like a shield, and he couldn't figure out a way to attack around it.

He gasped and sat up straight. Around! Could it be that simple? She had sidestepped anything that would bring her onto his turf, parried his approaches like a pro. Was he playing the wrong game?

"Quarterback sneak," he muttered.

"What's that, dear?"

"A football term," he told her absently, wondering why this hadn't occurred to him before. "The quarterback takes the ball himself and moves up the middle. Right through the defensive line." A wolfish grin spread across his face. "I'm beginning to like football."

"I think I'd better be going."

He glanced over at Amanda, who was chuckling. "What?"

"Predatory bulldozers are off my list forever, dear. The General is much more comfortable. And he's a marvelous dancer!"

J.D. smiled slowly. Time to remove more of the linebackers. "How is he at pulling strings?"

Nine

Charly listened to the droning buzz as J.D.'s phone rang for the seventeenth time. With a muffled curse she slammed the receiver into its cradle and spun into the kitchen, losing a slipper in the process. After refilling her mug so quickly the coffee slopped over the side, and she angrily gulped the hot liquid, scalding her tongue. She hissed in pain and tears rose to cloud her eyes, tears she brushed away with an impatient hand.

Damn the man, she thought. First he aggravates her, then he suddenly changes into a different person, then he loves her senseless, then he backs off . . . and then he disappears. When she'd called him the previous night, to apologize and invite him to her family dinner, she'd just assumed he'd gone out by himself. But all morning she'd gotten no answer at his hotel. Where was he? Had he met some bimbo on the beach? Lord knew, with his classic good looks he could have anyone he wanted.

She paled and gripped the edge of the counter, dizzied by the turn her wayward mind had taken. She was jealous! She was absolutely enraged at the thought of him with another woman! This had never happened to her before!

"Get a grip on yourself," she said sternly, her gaze on the dragon in front of her. "You can't be jealous. To be jealous, first you have to be in love." She nodded, gulped, and stood rigid, calming herself with her own logic. "But you aren't in love with him, because love makes you crazy. And you, my girl, are perfectly sane."

Ignoring the fact that she was talking to a dish towel, she gained courage from her own words. "I am not in love with him!" she announced to the empty kitchen. "I am still breathing, even though he's gone. My heart is still beating! I am . . . happy, yes, happy by myself!" She took a deep breath. "I am woman, hear me roar!"

Her shoulders slumped. "Good grief. I don't believe I said that."

Giggling, feeling much more herself, she went upstairs to shower and dress. The house echoed hollowly. Her brother and sister-in-law had left early to go to the military hospital's maternity clinic for Julia's regular checkup. She was grateful for the solitude, but without Aaron's irritating presence Charly found herself thinking about J.D.—again.

Her resolve firmed as she fluffed her damp hair. No, absolutely not. She would never be jerked around and turned into a baby factory by some male who would dump her at the first bad stretch of road. Or because of his stupid job. She would never allow herself to care for someone so deeply that his disappearance would make her walk around like a wraith for years, working herself into the ground just to support herself, smiling when she'd rather be crying because the children missed him as much as she did. Never. Not in a million, million years. She was smarter and stronger than that.

She pulled on her jeans with an impatient tug. J.D. was as loathesome as all others of his species. If he came back, she would spit on his Italian shoes and tell him to get another teacher. She had just retired.

Nodding, she marched downstairs, averting her eyes from the spotless living room on the way out the door and to school. The routine of setting up for the first day of classes would soothe her, calm her, like fingers rubbing her knotted neck. . . .

With an angry growl she rushed down the sidewalk, swept around the corner of her garage, and nearly collided with J.D.

"Charly!" He reached out to steady her by the shoulders, grinning. "Can't have another accident, can we?"

"You!" Her eyes narrowed. "You—you—*man!*" She spat the word.

Both of his dark brows shot up. "What did I do?"

"Where have you been?" Shoot, she thought, that wasn't what she'd meant to say at all.

"I went home to make some . . . arrangements."

She tossed her head. "I didn't care anyway." Remembering her earlier vow, she glanced at his feet, deflating somewhat as she saw his running shoes. But the second part of her plan she could still do, and do with a vengeance. Her fiery gaze returned to his. "I quit!"

"Teaching?"

"Yes!" She huffed. "No, not teaching school, just teaching you!"

"Good."

Poised for an argument, she found herself groping for words. "Huh?"

"I said good. I'm tired of being a student."

"Oh." A great emptiness opened up inside her,

and she fought it frantically. "Then I guess this is good-bye, right?"

His smile softened. "Hardly." He turned to bend into his Mercedes, glancing back over his shoulder. "Who trimmed your toast, anyway?"

"My—" She giggled nervously as a rush of heat raged in her body at the sight of his firm backside in tight jeans. "My what?"

"Your toast." He returned to his rummaging. "My mother used to trim the crust off my father's toast in the morning, just to see if it would make him angry. He hated trimmed toast."

"Did he?" She blinked. "Get mad, I mean."

"No. But she didn't stop trying." J.D. stood and turned to her, clutching two long, sharp objects in one hand and two wire-meshed things in the other. His green eyes warmed as he gazed at her. "I missed you."

"I—" She forced away all those spaghetti-bellied emotions he roused in her. "What do you have?"

"These?" He grinned wickedly. "Just a little challenge, Charly."

He tossed one of the long ones toward her, and she reflexively caught it, staring in astonishment. "A sword?"

"A foil to be exact. It's my turn. I'm going to teach you to fence."

As he strode past her she gaped first at him then at the foil, then back at his retreating form. "Wait a minute!" He didn't pause, so she hurried after him to the rear of her house. He was eyeing the redwood deck with a meditative frown on his face.

"It's a bit on the short side, but it'll do."

"What about my team?"

"You don't have to go until this afternoon."

"J.D., I don't *want* to learn to fence!"

"I know." He raised one brow and smiled. "But you will."

She held out the foil to him, her mouth set mutinously. His confidence irritated her. "No, I won't."

"I think you will. You forget, this is a challenge. I answered yours, you can answer mine."

"What are you talking about?"

"You said it was time I got out of my ivory tower, that my perspective was warped."

"I didn't say that!"

"Implied, granted." He held out a mesh mask. "I've proven that I can have fun your way. Now you need to return the same consideration. Or would you rather admit that you can't do this, that it's too difficult, and save us time."

She met his gaze defiantly. *He* was laughing at *her*! How dare he! "Give me that." She snatched the mask from his hand. "I can do anything I put my mind to."

"I know that, love. I just don't think you realize the power of that ability."

Her anger left her abruptly. He truly believed it. J.D. taunted her, but only to get her to accept his challenge. And she had to admit, those Errol Flynn movies they'd watched had peaked her interest.

"Stinker," she murmured. Her heart swelled, but before he could see the disconcerting emotions play across her face, she raised her brows and saluted him with her foil, mimicking some late-night swashbuckler.

He dodged as she nearly took off an ear. "I think we have a long way to go," he said with a sigh.

She giggled.

Though Charly wanted to leap right in with the actual parries, J.D. firmly told her she needed the basics first. Thankfully, her teacher's instincts affirmed his statement that she couldn't run before she walked, otherwise he had a horrible feeling he'd be missing several body parts if he allowed her to attack at will.

"I compete in all three areas—foil, épée, and saber. Fencing is one of the few sports that uses not only your body, but your mind in an almost religious definition. The day we met, you asked me about martial arts. In a way, this was Europe's version of kung fu."

"I just cannot see David Carradine with a sword."

He ignored her interruption. "You need judgment, quickness, precision, the glance, and the feel for the blade."

"The glance? Is that like the evil eye?"

"Yes."

"Oh."

That got her, he thought. "You need to concentrate on your opponent, on his body movements, and learn to anticipate his actions. That's part of football too. You watch, you shift with the other's motions, and you defeat."

"Do we get to pat each other's bottom in fencing?"

"I wish," he murmured, wanting to do more than pat her right now. Her comments were beginning to irritate him, but he figured that was her intention, so he decided to play the stern taskmaster, to force the interest he knew was there. Once Charly became involved with something, she tore into it like a rat terrier. Then, with her excuses gone, he would move in for the kill.

"This is the foil," he explained, holding up the object in question.

"No kidding."

"Charley!" He frowned at her, and she tried to look solemn. "It's composed of two portions—the blade and the handle—each of which is subdivided into several parts." He indicated the first third, from the tip downward. "This is the point. This is where the touch is made to your opponent. The middle, the next third, is where the blades touch during the engagement. And the heel, the lower third, is where the parries are executed. The steel that passes from the guard through the grip to the pommel is called the tongue."

She nodded. "From where the thrusts are executed." He shot her a dark look, and she giggled. "Sorry."

"Hold the handle loosely, thumb upward and nearly touching the guard, fingers underneath."

"Like a tennis racquet?"

"Almost. Your thumb and index finger will manage the foil, while your other fingers will control parrying. Your wrist plays the biggest part, but you use your whole body in the actual engagement." He grinned. "You're in good shape, darlin', but believe me, you'll find muscles you didn't even know you had tomorrow."

She pursed her mouth. "Go for it."

He taught her to keep her left foot flat on the ground at all times, which was essential to anchor her body and prevent uncoordinated movement. Once she was actually moving, her comments became less inhibiting to his teaching and were more to the point of learning. He showed her the correct salute, the positions of attention, on guard, the advance, the retreat—which she said she never did—correct arm extension, lunge, and recovery, forward and backward.

She was an apt pupil, but executed each of these with the stiffness inherent to first-time students. "Relax," he told her softly. "You need to flow smoothly, otherwise your executions will be jerky and easy to counter."

She took a deep breath. "I'm trying."

"I know. Try it again. Left leg stiff, lift your right foot only an inch or so and lunge forward, arm straight." She did, the point of her foil wobbling erratically. "No, love. Relax your hips. You're too tense." He positioned himself behind her and placed his hands on her waist, slipping one beneath her jeans to the small of her back to rub gently. "You're going to be in knots if you're not careful."

She straightened abruptly, bringing her ear nearly to his mouth. "Relax," he whispered. His heart leapt madly in his chest as he smelled the clean scent of her shampoo. He felt his arousal begin, slowly, achingly sweet, and slid his other hand around to her flat stomach. "You're doing just fine, love."

His mouth traced the curve of her ear seductively as he caressed her belly in slow circles. Beneath his fingertips, he felt her take a sharp breath, the muscles in her back unwinding. She tilted her head against his shoulder and he slipped both arms around her, drawing her buttocks firmly against his rapidly hardening manhood. He leaned forward, turning her face to his with a nudge of his chin, and kissed her.

She whimpered in pleasure not protest, and he slid his hand to her breast, cupping the fullness in his palm. His thumb found the pebbled nipple and rubbed slowly. Her breath quickened, and her tongue darted out to trace his mouth in a caress that sent his blood pressure skyrocketing.

After several aching moments of this torture, he pulled back, gazing into her passion-filled blue eyes. Heavy-lidded with desire, they answered his unspoken question with uncertainty, and he smiled crookedly. No matter how he'd thought to use her extraordinary responses against her, he couldn't take advantage of that vulnerable, little-girl confusion.

She was right, he thought with a sigh. Nobility stinks.

"Don't worry, love," he said, kissing the tip of her nose. "If you think the other night was a mistake, it won't happen again."

"It wasn't a mistake!" Her eyes widened as the words seemed to slip out. "I mean—"

"Shh . . ." He caressed her cheek and drew away, bending swiftly to retrieve their dropped weapons. At least he had her thinking, not attacking. That was more than he could wish for at this point. He glanced up at the lowering sun, surprised that so much time had passed. "Lesson's over, love. You have a lot of potential."

"Potential?"

He nodded and smiled at her. She stood where he had left her, her mouth still kiss-swollen, but the anguish had disappeared from her face. "You're a quick study, you're in excellent condition, and most of all, you have the reflexes of a cat. I think you have the makings of a master."

After a moment she eyed him suspiciously. "You're just saying that to make me drop my guard, aren't you?"

He stiffened. "No, Charly. I don't throw compliments around like confetti. And I don't use them to seduce women."

Rigid with indignation, he saluted her briefly, spun on his heel, and walked away. Why was it that he had to fall in love with the only woman who could enrage him with the simplest of statements? Or encourage him with the slightest of provocations?

Maybe because his guilty conscience told him that had been his intention in the first place.

"Trim my toast, will you?" he muttered with a

rueful chuckle, then he climbed in his car and sped away.

Late that night, J.D. lay staring at the moonlit ceiling, wondering if he would survive the rest of the week. Charly was a woman in every way. She was earth mother, child, partner. She was in turn endearing, aggravating, frustrating, and awe-inspiring. She would put him in the grave.

A soft knock startled him from his musings. He hesitated a moment, but grabbed his robe and belted it tightly before opening his door.

"Hi," said Charly, unusually subdued. She fidgeted with her jacket.

"Hi," he echoed. He held her gaze for a moment, then ushered her in. She smiled and entered, nervously darting glances around his darkened room. "Is something wrong?"

"No, not exactly. I mean—I was thinking—" She sighed and turned toward him. "Look, J.D. We're two mature adults, right?"

He nodded and closed the door.

"Right," she repeated. "After you left today, I decided that—I thought about what you said—" She took a deep breath. "I'm sorry I lashed out at you. I didn't mean what I said, at least not the way it sounded. And I think if we just admitted that we both want a sexual relationship, we wouldn't keep snarling at each other."

"I want more than that," he said quietly. "I love you."

Her eyes widened in panic. "This was a bad idea."

She bolted to the door, but he caught her by the arm. "Why are you afraid of that word, Charly? Don't you believe that I could love you?"

"That's a loaded question," she whispered. "If I

say yes, I sound arrogant. If I say no, I sound insecure."

"And you're neither." He turned her gently and tilted her chin up. "I love you, Charly. I don't know when it happened, or why, but I do. This isn't blackmail. It's a hazard."

Her brow creased in puzzlement.

"To throw oneself on the opponent's blade without turning it aside."

"Oh, J.D." Her eyes misted.

"I don't expect to hear it, honey. Not yet."

"What if it's never?"

His heart twisted, but her tone was not as firm as she tried to make it, and that gave him hope. "Tell me." Her eyes closed, and he kissed each lid. "Tell me why you can't, or won't even consider loving me too."

"Because . . ." She trailed away and a tiny droplet appeared beneath each lash. "It's a trap, J.D. Love is a trap designed to make you need someone, to care for them so much that you can't function by yourself anymore." She moaned, an animal sound of pain. "I see it all the time, the broken relationships, the floundering woman. I saw it with my own mother. When Dad left, it killed her. It just took her years for her body to die. I—I can't go through that."

His chest tightened, and he pulled her into his arms. "Good Lord," he whispered. "You really believe that."

"Yes." She drew a shaky breath and attempted to pull away. "Let me go."

"No." Her halfhearted struggling ceased, and he kissed the top of her head. "I love you, and I don't feel trapped. I don't feel any less of a person because of what I feel for you. If anything, I feel more."

"But you're not me."

"No." He drew back and gazed into her blurred

eyes. Her withdrawal was subtle, but he could feel it. "And you're not your mother any more than I'm my father." She opened her mouth, but no words came out. He ached for her. "Charly, I'm not going to push you, and I'm not going to lie and say I'll never leave you alone. I have no way of predicting my death, any more than you do."

He wiped her tears with his thumbs. "But I think you're selling yourself terribly short if you think that you'd fall apart if someone you loved left again. I don't need you for every breath I take, every thought I think. And neither do you. That's not a loving relationship, it's parasitical."

"I—" She buried her face in his shoulder. "I'm scared, J.D. I don't like being scared. It's a weakness."

"No, love. It's human. You scared the hell out of me at first."

She gave him a chuckle. "Me?"

"You. And you know it."

"I try harder than most people."

His hand swept over her back, caressing the slowly unwinding muscles. "Think about it, okay? That's all I ask."

Her breath quickened, and her fingers crept into his hair. "I don't want to think any more."

She was parrying again, but she was still there. "You're just saying that to make me drop my guard," he said lightly.

"Nope. Just your robe."

His lips twitched. "You're a formidable opponent, Dragon Lady."

"I'm a quick study."

Their gazes locked. There was no battle of wills, no combat, no confusion to prompt his nobility. When Charly knew what she wanted, he thought ruefully, she didn't dance around the issue, she didn't feint to fool him into a counterattack. She lunged straight for the heart.

He smiled. "I admit it."

"What?"

"That I want at least a sexual relationship."

She smiled, a slow, sensual smile that accelerated his pulse. "So do I."

Their mouths met halfway, sweetly confirming the truth of their statements.

This time, when she left his bed in the wee hours of the night, J.D. said nothing, tried to quell his pain. He sensed that it was difficult for her, but he had no wish to arouse that panic and fear in her again. The last of her defenses had clicked in, and he wondered when, or even if, she would let them fall.

But he knew one thing clearly. When Charly spent the night in his arms, it wouldn't be the end. It would be their true beginning.

Ten

Charly opened her eyes, blinked, then smiled as memory intruded through the morning fuzziness. Yawning, she stretched languorously, wincing as her muscles protested. J.D. was wrong, she thought. Fencing used *most* of her body, but it was the athletics during the night that had finished her off.

But it was a wonderful ache, she decided as she stretched again. Her breasts felt heavy against the sheets, her neck and chest burned lightly from the rough caress of the whiskers of J.D.'s unshaven face.

All in all, it was not a bad way to start the day.

The fleeting realization that it would be better if she were to awaken next to that unshaven face she shoved from her thoughts. She refused to feel either guilt or longing. In spite of his declaration, everything was still on her terms. Exactly as she wanted it.

Rising from the bed proved more difficult than she'd guessed as her sore right thigh hurt from her energetic lunging in practice the previous day. But she had felt worse after a football game, and after a warm shower she could ignore even the worst of her pain. When J.D. returned to show her the different quadrants and lines of the opponent's body, she wouldn't shrink and complain like some wimp. She would show him that she was made of sterner stuff!

On impulse, she donned shorts and a T-shirt and ran down the beach to get him. At his door, she fought to control her labored breathing and knocked. It was opened immediately by a fully dressed J.D. His slow smile caused her thoughts to tangle into a great big mess.

"Good morning," he murmured, and claimed her mouth with his. Fire swept over her, but the demands of her body overpowered her desire. As she struggled for air, he relented, laughed, and ushered her in. "Do you want some water? Coffee? Oxygen?"

"Coffee." She groaned the word, leaping at his room service table like a starving woman. Before she could gulp from the cup she poured, he stayed her hand with a glass of orange juice.

"Sip it. You won't burn your mouth with this."

Remembering what she'd done the previous morning, she complied, and slowly her breathing returned to normal. With a heartfelt sigh, she sank into a chair and stretched her legs before her, glaring at her betrayers. "I think I'm getting old," she announced disgustedly.

"Senility is usually the first sign," he agreed.

She scowled at him. "I'm not senile."

"Only an insane woman would run after all the activities of yesterday." He grinned. "Or a very determined one."

"Determined." She nodded. "I like that word better." She chuckled, a sound mixed with a moan, and she slid lower into the chair. "I hurt all over! I thought it would be easier! How do you do this three times a week?"

His brows raised in an exaggerated expression of innocence. "I don't 'do it' three times a week. At least not until I met you."

Her eyes narrowed. "Fencing."

"Oh, that! I *fence* four times a week. But I've been doing it since I was sixteen." His smile softened. "If it's any consolation, my muscles ached after that workout you gave me on the beach with the football."

She smiled. "It helps. Thanks." Quickly, before she lost her momentum, she stood. "So, teach, what's on the agenda today? Do I get to aim at you or what?"

"No. Patience, love. You've only had one lesson. Finish your coffee."

"If I sit back down, I'll freeze that way." She walked to the door and beckoned to him. "Race you back."

Shaking his head, J.D. followed, carrying the foils. He wasn't surprised to find her waiting on the beach. "I couldn't leave you behind," she told him with mock concern. "Not with your heavy load and everything."

"Uh-huh."

She chuckled at his suspicious tone and snaked an arm around his waist. She felt comfortable with him, she realized. She'd had friends before, even one who had become a lover, but never had she had this sense of well-being with anyone. It had nothing to do with his feelings for her; this was all on her part. And for some reason, it didn't feel as frightening by the light of day. Even his unconscious little endearments didn't make her clench up inside anymore.

Sighing, she purposely mismatched her steps with J.D. and giggled as he strove to match them. By the time they reached her house, both were laughing playfully.

"I really do need my morning dose of coffee," she told him as they walked to her door. She paused, spun, and grabbed his shoulders, her expression stern. "Just brace yourself."

Confused, J.D. frowned. "For what?"

Holding his gaze, she threw open her door. "For my worst nightmare."

He glanced beyond her, and his jaw dropped. "What happened?" He passed her and stared around at her tidy living room, the neatly ordered ranks of books and dragons, neatly stacked magazines, the brightly polished furniture. J.D. couldn't remember her house ever being really dirty, but it had always looked like a hurricane had hit it. Until now. "It's—it's—"

"Blinding?" she supplied as she closed the door. "Some people chain-smoke when they're nervous, some people bite their nails. Julia cleans. I heard her down here again last night around three. She even dusted my computer, key by key with a dry watercolor brush. Eerie, huh?" She gave a quick rendition of *The Twilight Zone* theme. "You open a door and—"

"I thought I heard someone." A tiny redhead blinked sleepily and paced down the staircase. "Hi, Charly. You must be the infamous J. D. Smith." She seemed to glide to him, her hand outstretched. "I'm Julia. My, you're not nearly as ugly as some of the stories led on. And I do believe you have all your own teeth too. How disappointing."

J.D. stifled his astonishment with manners drilled into him from childhood and clasped her hand firmly. Like her pretty face, her hand was covered with freckles. Julia's accent was faintly British, and he remembered Charly's saying something about her being a military brat. Though only five feet tall, she radiated a warmth he found hard to resist. "Is someone spreading tales about me?"

"According to David, you have lecherous designs on Charly."

"But I do."

Her brown eyes opened wide, then she chuckled. "I like that in a man."

"Where's Aaron?" asked Charly quickly.

"On post," said Julia placidly, her twitching left eye the only sign of disturbance. "He received a phone call about a half an hour ago from the Department of Defense, then rushed out without a word."

J.D. stiffened slightly, but Charly was the only one to notice—and wonder.

Julia went on, "The only reason I'm not scrubbing your kitchen floor with a toothbrush is that he seemed happy about something. I thought someone had possibly broken your boyfriend's legs." Julia looked him over. "But he seems in perfect working order."

"Oh, that he is, Julia," Charly commented with a twinkle in her eyes.

"Good. Then I shall retire back to my spinning bed."

"Would you like some breakfast?"

Julia turned a delicate shade of green. "No, thank you, Charity. I shall stick to my tea."

As she crept slowly back up the stairs J.D. smiled, hoping, for Julia's sake, that Amanda's general had had something to do with Aaron's sudden excitement. It would give him a lot of pleasure to see a smile on her face. "I like her. Your brother's luckier than he knows." Then a thought hit him. A tiny frown creased his brow. What had Julia said?

"Oh, he knows all right. That's why he's so upset about this trans—"

J.D. turned startled eyes to Charly as Julia's words sunk in.

"—fer . . ." she finished weakly.

To his astonishment, a blush crept into her cheeks. "Charity?" he whispered.

"It's my name," she shot back through clenched teeth.

"Is this the real reason you didn't want me to meet them?"

Defiantly, she tilted her chin and glared at him. "So?"

His mouth quivered as he gathered her into his arms. "My name is John," he told her with as much solemnity as he could muster.

It took her a moment, but suddenly her blue eyes lit with amusement. "John Smith?"

"The Fourth," he said.

Valiantly, she fought her instinctive reaction. "I like J.D. better," she said. Her voice broke, and she cleared her throat. "As in 'juvenile delinquent.' "

"Oh, I don't know. I think Charity suits you to a tee." He kissed her before either could break into laughter, but it didn't work. Their lips curved at the same moment, and they shared something even more momentous than a bed.

Their fencing lesson was hardly J.D.'s rigid instructor's idea of proper. Lingering caresses punctuated his description of body quadrants, sudden bursts of amusement broke into concentration, and stolen kisses inhibited relaxed movement. Even so, he told her at the end of the session, she was progressing.

Charly promptly progressed down his chin to his chest.

Giggling, exchanging wicked, whispered taunts, they entered the house arm in arm sometime after noon. Telling him she had to kick off her shoes, Charly poised herself beside the closet, braced for the tumble. But when she threw open the door, she froze.

"What's wrong?" he asked, instantly concerned.

"Those spiders were my friends." Her voice quivered dramatically. "The woman's a murderer!"

He looked over her shoulder into the perfectly ordered closet. "Life is hard," he told her.

In spite of their other activities, both had worked up a sweat with their practice in the warmth of the sun. Standing in Charly's kitchen beside the washer, J.D. declared that he needed a shower and his clothes needed one too. He then proceeded to unbutton his shirt, his dancing green eyes holding Charly's as they widened in astonishment.

"J.D.," she whispered. "Julia's upstairs."

"No, she's not." He stripped off his damp shirt and tossed it into the machine. "I heard her leave about an hour ago."

Charly's blood pulsed through every inch of her body as her gaze lingered on his tightly muscled chest. "You heard the door," she said without conviction. "You don't know if she left."

"Do you hear anyone in the house?" He unzipped his jeans.

Her tongue darted out to moisten suddenly dry lips as he pushed his pants down his legs. This quiet striptease was driving her crazy. "No. But that doesn't mean they couldn't come back at . . . at the crucial moment."

"That's true," he agreed as he peeled off his socks. "We'll have to hurry."

Charly groaned. His masculinity was clearly outlined by the thin fabric of his red briefs, and she almost relented. "Brothers are worse than grunion," she whispered. "They'd interrupt, I just know it." When he approached her with a wicked smile on his face, she turned away with a growl of pure frustration and clenched her fist on the counter. "Go take your shower."

He nuzzled her neck. "Join me?"

It was too much for her feeble willpower. "Okay. I'll start the washer and be up in a minute." She turned and gave him a lingering kiss. "I like it hot," she whispered.

"Don't I know it," he muttered, then took the stairs two at a time.

She watched him, stunned by the power of her attraction. The man had turned her into an addict, and she wondered if her cravings for him would ever be as easy to kick as chocolate had been. When she heard the water begin, she shook herself and pulled her socks off. Her shorts were next, but as she began to pull off her shirt, she heard the creak of the stairs.

"Patience," she called. "Get back in the bathroom, you sex maniac."

"I'll admit that's what got me into my present condition. But I hardly think Aaron would tell tales."

Shocked, Charly spun to find Julia on the step, regarding her with a wide grin. She made a grab for her shorts. "I thought you'd gone!"

"Aaron came home. He's asleep." Her face positively glowed as she rushed toward Charly and hugged her tightly. "His orders were changed back, Charity! Can you believe it? We're staying here!"

Charly gaped at her sister-in-law, thanking heaven she had fought her urges. Otherwise Julia might have been far more stunned than she. "But—how—"

"Someone called the Inspector General to begin an inquiry. It wasn't Aaron's fault!"

Warmed by Julia's happiness, Charly returned the embrace, momentarily forgetting J.D. "Oh, Julia. I'm so happy for you!"

"He'll be here when the baby comes, and I—" She sobbed. "I was so afraid of being alone for the birth. Now, he—" She drew back and wiped her tears away. "Sorry. I'm not usually such a—a watering pot."

"Honey, if anyone has a right to be, you do. But how did this happen? I thought Aaron cussed out a colonel!"

"He was merely defending one of his men, and he was not insubordinate. Your brother is a lot of things, Charity, but he is no fool." She sniffed. "When his orders were changed to Korea, we had no way of proving that it was an act of pure malice by his commanding officer. We couldn't even begin an investigation for fear it would look like Aaron was simply whining about his new post. But someone else did it!" She sighed. "Whoever it was, I will always be eternally grateful."

"Me, too, honey." Tears misted Charly's eyes. "And I get to see my niece—"

A muted bellow cut her words off. She glanced at the ceiling, suddenly remembering J.D.

"Aaron," whispered Julia. "I forgot all about him. I think he's just met your J.D."

"Oh, hell," Charly muttered, and made an automatic grab for her clothes.

A small herd of buffaloes seemed to clatter down the stairs, stopping her in her tracks. "Charly!" her brother yelled, "there's a naked man in your bathroom!"

Charly strove to remain calm. "Do you expect him to wear his clothes in there?" she asked reasonably, wondering if J.D. would need X rays.

"He's out now." Aaron's tone was strange.

Her eyes narrowed. "If you've hurt him, I'll—"

"I didn't touch him!" Dazed, Aaron frowned. "I yelled right into his face and he just said, 'You must be Aaron. I'm J.D.' Then he shook my hand and soaped his arms."

Charly bit her lip. That poker face of J.D.'s sure came in handy. Maybe she should cultivate one herself.

"Hello to you, too, darling." Julia wove her arms

around her husband's waist, and his face softened as he kissed her.

"Charly!" called J.D. "Do you have a robe?"

Charly giggled. "I'd better get him something, or he's likely to come downstairs in the buff."

"I'll do it," Aaron said. "He's probably in the buff right now."

"Aaron—" she began, but the stubborn set of his jaw stopped her. "I don't have one that'll fit him."

"I do." He stomped upstairs.

"He blusters and he bellows," Julia said with a laugh. "But he likes him. I can tell. Aaron hates cringers."

"Right."

"Don't worry, Charity. We'll be out of your way tonight."

"Right," she muttered again absently. She had just remembered something about J.D.'s attitude earlier when Julia had mentioned Aaron's excitement this morning. It hadn't hit her before, but J.D.'s poker face hadn't quite functioned that time. He hadn't butted in again, not after he knew how she felt about it!

Had he?

Julia shook her gently by the shoulder, and she brought herself back to reality. "Huh?"

"I said, why don't you and J.D. join us for a celebratory dinner?"

Charly smiled grimly. "I don't think that's such a good idea. I don't want to spoil it for you." Like with a little murder, she added silently.

"Ah! You want to be alone."

"No witnesses," Charly muttered under her breath.

Julia frowned, her mind once again on her own problems. "I'd better find something for Aaron to wear. The army is perfect in that respect—he has no choice. It's either his uniform or his uniform. Civilian clothing baffles him."

Before she took a step, Aaron hurried back down the stairs, buttoning a yellow shirt over ocher slacks. Julia winced, then diplomatically suggested they leave early. Aaron frowned at his sister, but his wife's pleading softened him in a way that Charly had never been able to, and he agreed.

Once they'd left, Charly stormed the stairs. She found J.D. in her bedroom, only partially dressed. Ignoring the warmth that blossomed inside her, she crossed her arms over her chest and shot from the hip.

"Did you have anything to do with my brother's sudden change of orders?"

J.D.'s hand froze in the act of buttoning his shirt just for a moment, then he continued. "Yes."

Charly's anger blazed, and she felt a sharp stab of pain. "You stuck your nose in my business again!"

"He needed help." He lifted his gaze from his task, his green eyes unwavering. "I could give it. You couldn't. It was as simple as that."

"I didn't ask for your help!"

"You didn't need it."

"That's not the point!"

"That's exactly the point. Your brother was in the bind, not you. And my mother is dating a retired general who was absolutely delighted to help."

Her nostrils flared, and she took a deep breath, attempting to quell her hurt. "And Hogan's art scholarship?"

"I didn't do anything you wouldn't have done yourself, if you'd known the right people. I haven't interfered in your business at all. You handled Hogan, Melissa, the razing of those shacks. I just opened doors a couple of times. The truth did the rest."

"Words. Tactics. You're good with those, aren't

you, J.D." she turned away, clenching her fists. Tears stung her eyes. "What about your speech last night, huh? Does 'sharing' mean anything to you?"

"It means everything to me. I love you, but this wasn't about you. Would you keep them from their happiness just because your pride got in the way?"

Charly closed her eyes and shuddered. She'd never thought about it that way. "You could have told me."

He moved up behind her and touched her shoulder. She flinched away, but he persisted. "If I would have, what would you have done?"

"Told you to go to he—heck."

"Exactly." He brushed aside her hair and kissed the sensitive spot below her ear. "And could you have done either of those things yourself?"

His warm breath sent shivers up her spine. His rationalization drained her fury as his touch eroded her pain. "You didn't give me the chance to find out."

"You're absolutely right." His tongue trailed along the chord of her neck.

"Don't do that," she murmured, her tone belying her words.

"What?"

"Kiss me."

"I like to kiss you."

"We're arguing, dammit!"

"No, you're arguing. I'm agreeing."

Why couldn't he yell back at her? What power did he have over her that she couldn't even find the tiniest spark of anger left? "You're cheating," she whispered desperately.

"I'm equalizing." Then his hands turned her, and his mouth found hers.

Charly wondered if she'd ever understand him, or herself, as she gave in to the sensations.

• • •

A long time later, she lay on her stomach, utterly sated, as J.D. blew warm kisses all over her back. She chuckled suddenly. "The grunion have run," she murmured.

"On the other side of the beach." He traced her spine to the small of her back. "Leaving the mice to play."

"That's a cat," she said thickly. "You're mixing your metaphors."

"Sue me." He paused, then stiffened suddenly. "Charly," he said in a strange tone. "I thought you hated roses."

So he had finally found the last of her secrets. She stifled the panic that thought brought. "I dislike men who think roses can solve problems."

"I don't suppose this"—his fingers tickled a spot just above her left hip—"has anything to do with the reason you reacted so strongly."

"Uh-uh. I like roses."

"So I see. When did you do this?"

"Prom night. I didn't have a date, so some of us got together and did some . . . rather foolish things."

"But a rose?"

"I guess I'm a closet romantic."

"A rose tattoo, huh?"

She rolled toward him, twining her arms around his neck, distracting him in the most pleasurable way she could think of. "Are you shocked?"

"You can't shock me anymore. The unexpected is the norm."

"I think I like that."

"You're not going to let me stay with you tonight, are you?"

She stiffened. "No. I can't."

"Why?"

Because I'm falling in love with you.

Her throat closed over the words as her mind shoved away the thought.

"Let's go eat," she said, and exited the room before he could say a word.

Eleven

For the next three days Charly could think of nothing else but her feelings for J.D and the confusion they caused. It distracted her during football practice, it intruded into her conversations with her brother and friends, and it caught her unawares in the deepest part of the night as she lay alone in her bed. The only time she *didn't* feel this internal battle was when she was with him. Usually. This time was different.

"Parry!" he cried.

"That *was* a parry." She growled and struck "on guard." The white, padded tunic he had provided was beginning to make her swelter in the sun's warmth, but she ignored the discomfort. It was the first time he had allowed her to actually aim at him, and she wanted to enjoy it.

J.D. thrust high, and Charly bounced the tip of his foil aside, her heart swelling with pride as he glowed his approval.

"Good! Good! Tierce!"

"Bless you."

He chuckled. "That particular parry was called

tierce. Fingernails downward, eye-level point, hand and wrist articulation pronounced."

"And here I thought I was just shoving it out of the way."

He frowned thoughtfully. "Maybe I should have taught you the names of all of them and their correct executions." He nodded. "Prime, seconde, tierce, quarte, quinte, sixte, septime, and octave are all used to parry a particular thrust . . ."

Charly groaned, but smiled softly at the excitement on his face as he demonstrated each one.

When they were together, whether during these incessant drills he insisted upon or just walking on the beach, Charly sensed a heightened awareness of everything around her. The sun shone brighter, the birds sang louder, and the air smelled sweeter. It was nothing that he did, for he acted no differently than he always had. His wry sense of humor, his touching nobility, his slow smile, even his aloof observation of others, were all the same. It was she who had changed. And she wasn't sure she liked it.

She had always considered herself a strong woman, one who didn't need the kind of caring that J.D. showed her. It was more than the massage of aching muscles after a workout, more than the deepening passion they had discovered in the bedroom. It was the amusement they exchanged with a glance across a group of people, a reminder of some private joke an inadvertent comment had prompted. It was the heart-stopping lack of breath she experienced when J.D. simply brushed a strand of hair from her cheek. It was the darkening of his green eyes that she could prompt with merely a smile, the rumbling laughter she could feel through her bones when she tried to antagonize him.

It was the intimacy, the *sharing*, that frightened her. Because she was very much afraid that if she gave too much away, she wouldn't have anything left.

"Okay," he was saying. "If I make a thrust into low quarte"— he aimed toward the left side of her rib cage—"you what?"

Charly turned her wrist and nails downward, keeping her foil horizontal, and crossed his foil, slapping it aside. "I quinte."

"Very good. I wasn't sure you were listening." He lifted their masks, kissed her on the tip of her nose, and replaced them. "Now let's try that same thrust with a septime parry."

She huffed, but readied herself.

Maybe he pushed so hard because this was their last real day together. The thought caused her heart to fall straight through to her toes. Tomorrow was her party to celebrate the new team and the beginning of school, and Tuesday he would return to San Francisco. His imminent departure intensified her confusion, as if she had accidentally put all of her emotions in a blender and he had switched it up a couple of notches. Because she didn't know what was going to happen next, and he hadn't brought it up.

"You're not concentrating," J.D. told her sternly as her point wobbled past his arm. "You can do these, Charly. I know you can. You're the best student I've ever had."

She attempted a rueful smile and was glad he couldn't see beneath her fencing mask as she failed. "I'm the only student you ever had."

"True, love, but that doesn't make you any less apt."

"Don't call me that," she snapped, irritated with herself.

He removed his mask. "Are you worried about the team's chances this season?"

There it was again, his easy concern about something that was usually her territory alone. Since their confrontation, since her outrage at his interference, he had used that same angle with her. Not only did he tell her of his family, his goals in life, he had begun to draw the same information from her. And what could she do? She had opened her big mouth!

"No, the team's fine." She struck on guard. "Let's try again."

He sighed and replaced his mask.

His thrusts continued to be slow and focused, but Charly found herself using more and more force to slap him away. He stabbed into the high quarte, and she countered, a circular parry he had only told her about. But he said nothing and attacked again. Charly used her entire arm to heave his foil aside. Before he even struck on guard, she lunged at him and touched him with the point of her foil.

"Illegal," he murmured with no reproach. "But cute. Let's try again."

With a deep breath Charly forced her anguish deep down inside and tried to focus on the lesson. But it wasn't easy. Chaos reigned in her mind and her body, but she could hardly tell him that. On the one hand, every time she saw him, she wanted to see more of him. His humor and pure masculinity stirred her as no other man's had. He was the kind of lover she'd never dreamed existed, tender and gentle yet with a hungry passion that had overwhelmed her.

Yet on the other hand, she wanted him out of her life, because that very joy threatened her in a way she'd never experienced. His high-handedness infuriated her. Yet it was this very strength that had attracted her in the first place, the strength to carry burdens far heavier than hers, and his own as well. The strength to do battle with her on an equal basis, without his male ego overcompensating and trying to deny her own freedom of choice. He was no petulant little boy, no Peter Pan wishing to never grow up, no strutting rooster blatantly showing his physical power over her. He was, basically, the complete opposite of every man she'd ever known.

Her concentration shot, the point of her foil nearly gouged him in the throat. He removed his mask and frowned at her, the tiny lines between his brows endearing as he chided her gently.

Damn the man! If he would only become predictable, it would make things so much easier. Because she did respect him, his character, his strong will. Was this love? she wondered.

She just didn't know anymore.

But she did know that she had never thanked him, and it suddenly became imperative that she did. "J.D., I need to tell you something—"

"No!" His vehemence stunned her into silence. "Not now."

He moved forward and she pressed the tip of her foil against the pristine white of his chest. It bent as he ignored it. "I wanted to thank you for helping my brother," she said. "And everything."

"Oh." One corner of his mouth lifted. "Don't worry about it."

"What did you think I was going to say?"

"It's not important." Gingerly, he removed the obstacle and reached out to remove her mask and drop it to the deck. His hand fluffed her damp, flattened hair, and his gaze studied her mutinous expression. "I think it's time for a reward."

Her blood heated, but her eyes narrowed. "Uh-huh. A reward for whom?"

"You. I'm taking you to dinner tonight."

"Oh?" His thumb traced her mouth, and her breathing became ragged. "Don't I have a choice in this?"

"Nope. Not this time." He kissed her slowly, his tongue making delicate forays along her lips. "You've done so much for me, love. Let me do something nice for you for a change."

She melted against him. When he put it like that, he was difficult to resist. Her arms crept around his neck, and she placed her forehead against his. "You've taught me to fence. Isn't that nice enough?"

"What? Did I hear that right? She's actually admitting that she likes it?"

"Stinker." Her gaze held his. "I like it, J.D. I never imagined it would be so tough, and I never imagined it would be so much fun. It is the sport of kings, not the sport of wimps. Are you happy now?"

He pressed against her. "I love a woman who can admit she's wrong."

"Don't push it." In spite of herself, she giggled, and her mouth captured his in a passionate kiss that sent her pulse racing.

He broke it off with a groan. "We'll never get there if you do that again."

"Oh, well," she murmured, but he backed away.

"I have something else for you, if you'll wear them tonight."

"Don't tell me you found me a T-shirt that says 'Fencing masters thrust better.' "

"No, but it's a thought. Besides, I said 'them' not 'it.' "

Sighing, she allowed him to lead her to his bag at the edge of the deck. He rummaged through it and lifted out a small box. She frowned. "What is it?"

He placed it in her hand, a hesitant smile on his face. "Open it."

She gasped when she saw a pair of sapphire earrings nestled in the velvet lining. "I can't wear these!"

"Sure you can." He turned one over. "See? They're clips. I noticed you don't have pierced ears."

"I used to, but I let all the holes grow closed," she said absently. "J.D., these are the size of Iowa!"

"No, they're not. 'All' the holes? How many did you have?"

"Six." She peeped up at him through her lashes, attempting to cover the fact that his gift had touched her deeply. "In each ear."

He blinked. "Why did you let them close?"

"Have you ever tried to sleep with those sharp little points pressing into your neck?"

"Uh, no."

She cocked her head, her eyes dancing. "Maybe . . ." She touched his lobe. "You know, you'd look great with an earring. Maybe just a little diamond stud—"

He grabbed her hand and laughed as he kissed her. "I'll stud you . . ." When their bodies were entwined once again, he asked her softly, "Will you accept them? And wear them tonight?"

"Sure." Charly could deny him nothing, not when he was so eager for her to like them. Later in the evening they could discuss the problems of a long-distance relationship, but she realized that she wanted to take the next step. She just wished she knew what that was. "I'd be honored."

"And a special dress? Or do you—"

"Don't worry," she said quickly. "I have something just perfect."

She kissed him slowly, frantically wondering when the stores closed.

J.D. had showered, shaved, and dressed in his dark suit, all the while unable to erase the frown from his face. Charly's performance earlier had been totally out of character. She had something on her mind, and he had no doubt it was their relationship. The question was, what had she decided in these last days of wrestling with the problem?

He absentmindedly tied his tie backward twice before he swore and threw it to the floor, only recovering it because he was running late. He raked his hair with his hand, then combed it back. He was dawdling, and he realized it was because he didn't know what she was going to do.

Charly was the only person he'd never been able to read clearly. Her tense body language and volatile attitude told him one thing, but her melting sweetness told him another. He had the horrible feeling that she would walk out one minute, and the wonderful feeling that she would never leave the next.

He hated this. One way or the other, they had to settle things. He wouldn't end it. And he didn't want to give her the opportunity to either. If he had to drive down every day from San Francisco to see her, to continue their relationship, he would. She was far too precious to lose.

When J.D. picked Charly up that night, the glow that warmed his eyes when he saw her told her more than words ever could. His gaze sent goose bumps popping out all over her skin, and she was glad she could shock him after all. Pride filled her as she walked arm in arm with him into his hotel's restaurant, trying desperately not to give herself away by hobbling on the unfamiliar heels. But panic overtook pride as the meal drew to a close. What was happening to her? Was this what love did?

J.D. gazed at her in the candlelight, still astonished at her transformation but refusing to let her see just how much it had stunned him. Her lovely brown hair, held back at the temples with combs, tumbled around her shoulders. The sapphire earrings glittered in the reflected light. Her gown was simply tailored. The plunging neckline emphasized the fullness of her breasts, and the swirling hem flattered her beautifully shaped legs. Her high-heeled shoes had nearly brought her eye to eye with him.

She was striking, magnificent, and carried her height proudly. "You are incredible," he said reverently.

She self-consciously fidgeted with her padded shoulders. "When are normal clothes going to come back? I look like Lyle Alzado."

He cocked his head. "You don't have a beard. Maybe you should grow one."

Surprise, then delight lit her eyes. "You always know just what to say to a girl, don't you, Mr. Smith?"

"Of course, Ms. Czerniowski. That color is perfect on you," he said. "It brings out the red highlights in your hair and the violet in your eyes."

"You don't know how lucky you are. I nearly bought another wonderful little number—tight black skirt, yellow-and-black-striped tube top with pull-on matching sleeves."

He tried to picture it and enjoyed the image he saw. "Like a torch dancer from fifties Paris."

"Is that what they were called where you come from? We have another name for them."

"You'd look beautiful in whatever you wore."

She lowered her gaze. "We need to talk, J.D. About us."

"I don't think this is the time."

"It hasn't been the time all evening," she muttered.

"Not tonight." He had cut her off several times already, but he didn't want to hear the words that would end their relationship. She loved him. She was just too stubborn to admit it. He had seen her distraction all evening, and he absolutely refused to give her the opportunity.

He would use her own bulldog tactics on her! By keeping her off balance, he would win the game.

"Would you like dessert? To go dancing? Either of the above?"

"No, I—" She cleared her throat. "I have something to say."

His mouth went dry. "No."

Her brows raised. "No, what?"

"No, I don't want to hear it."

"Will you stop that! You don't even know what I was going to say!"

His jaw firmed. "We're not going to spoil this evening with a fight."

She gaped at him. "Then don't start one!"

"That's it." He stood abruptly, knocking over his chair in the process, and grabbed her wrist. "We're going to have this out. In private."

Charly gasped as he dragged her to her feet. "What's wrong with you?"

"Nothing," he said grimly, and tugged. "I'm just playing your game for a change."

Numb with astonishment, Charly matched his energetic stride, or tried to. Her shoes seemed to have a mind all their own. And he wouldn't let go of her! "Slow down!" she cried. "Dammit, J.D., stop! I can't run in heels!"

He paused long enough to peel off her shoes and toss them at the shocked maître d'. "Keep the change," he told him, then swung Charly up into his arms, glaring at her. "You owe the bucket a dollar."

"I—" She gulped once—hard—at his expression. He strode to the elevator, rigid with fury, and she didn't know whether to laugh or punch his lights out.

Laughter won. He scowled at her as she struggled to subdue the giggles that rose to her throat. She knew that if she applied the slightest pressure on some of his more sensitive parts he'd drop her like a hot potato. But since he seemed to be going in the right direction—his room—she did nothing. It should have occurred to her before that J.D. might think she was ready to end their relationship instead of to work out how to continue it. Heaven knew she'd had enough hints throughout the day. He would pay for his romantic impetuosity soon enough.

"Barbarian," she muttered under her breath, and made herself go completely limp, letting gravity take its course.

By the time they were in his room, she could feel his muscles trembling from the strain of her not extreme but imposing dead weight. It set her off again, and J.D. glowered at her as he dropped her feet to the floor. "You're not exactly Scarlett O'Hara," he muttered, rolling his shoulders.

She pressed her lips together. "It does look easier in the movies, doesn't it?" She sat on the edge of his bed, folding her hands primly in her lap. "Now, you wanted to have something out?"

"Yes, I—" He took a deep breath. "It's about what you wanted to say."

She tried to compose herself. "Yes, J.D.?" When he paused, she encouraged him. "Come on, keep up the momentum."

"Don't do that! This isn't something to laugh about!"

"Yes, J.D." Her expression was solemn, but her lungs nearly burst with the effort of holding back her amusement. He was so beautiful when he was angry. And her placid appearance obviously disconcerted him.

Sternly, he went nose to nose with her. "We have a good relationship."

"Yes, J.D."

"And I'm not talking about just sexually either. We're opposites, but we complement each other. We dovetail. Separately, we're fine. Together we're stronger."

That much was true, she thought, but wouldn't allow her face to soften. "Yes, J.D."

"I love you."

"Yes, J.D."

"And you love me!"

Her breath caught in her throat. "Yes, J.D."

"You're just too stub—" He blinked. "What did you say?"

"I said, 'Yes, J.D.' " Her eyes filled with moisture, and her voice lowered huskily. "I said I love you."

"You love me," he repeated blankly, then his face lit up like a sunrise. "And you're going to marry me."

She took a deep, steadying breath. "No, J.D."

J.D.'s face fell for a moment, then a rueful grin spread across his mouth. "I knew it was too good to be true."

"I love you," she repeated firmly.

"I love you too." He smiled and kissed her softly. "To be honest, I wasn't sure that much would happen."

She ran her hands up his chest and began to unbutton his jacket. "Never underestimate your abilities. Isn't that what you told me?"

"Something like that." His green eyes darkened as she started in on his shirt. "If it's a matter of your job and mine, we can choose some neutral ground, like San Jose. That's about halfway between the two."

She paused. "Let me get used to loving you first, okay?" Her unconsciously pleading gaze told him of her uncertainty better than words could. "Please?"

He gathered her into his arms and pulled her beside him on the bed. "This isn't how it was supposed to go," he muttered.

"Yes, J.D." Impishly, she one-handedly continued her task.

"I was supposed to storm your defenses."

"Yes, J.D."

"Well, nothing else worked. I thought you were going to put an end to us completely."

"I know."

His laughter held a note of triumph. "But it's just the beginning. Everything will work out now." His breathing became ragged as she ran her fingers over the hair on his chest. "You're going to spend the night here, aren't you."

It wasn't a question, but she answered it as she feathered kisses over his ear. "Yes, J.D."

"Will you stop that? I feel as if I've stepped into a movie about pod people, or something."

She giggled. "Yes, J.D."

He rolled her over and frowned at her. "Do you think I'm trying to trap or change you? I'm not, love."

"I know."

"You're a hellion, and I don't want anything different."

"And you are trying to be a stereotype." She quickly reversed their positions and straddled him, unbuckling his pants. "Men," she muttered disgustedly. "They never know when to shut up."

He grinned. "Yes, Charly."

Neither spoke another word.

Twelve

Charly awoke slowly the next morning. She experienced no abrupt jerk into reality, no lingering feeling that something was amiss, just a floating, subtle awareness of everything around her. J.D.'s clean scent tickled her nostrils, mixed with the musky fragrance of their lovemaking. Her head was cushioned on firm, warm muscle instead of yielding down. Her body ached pleasantly all over.

Her mouth curved into a smile. Without opening her eyes, she snuggled into J.D.'s body, and his arm tightened around her. Why had this frightened her so much? she wondered. How could anything that felt so good be bad for her?

She would miss him this week while he was in San Francisco. The thought intruded into her happiness, but she didn't draw away. He had become more than a part of her life, he had become a part of her. Of course she would miss him, just as she'd miss an arm if it were gone. He was right about their dovetailing. He had become an anchor for her recklessness, and she had drawn him out of his "objective" cocoon. They brought out the best in each other. What could be wrong about that?

There would be nothing shameful in missing him, she realized. The shame would be in her falling apart because of it. But she wouldn't. Suddenly, there was no doubt in her mind that although she would miss him, she would survive.

Her mouth went dry. For once in her life, Charly didn't want everything to happen too fast, as he obviously did. She needed to wait, to see if she was right. She wasn't certain she could live with such a strong personality. When her life was back to normal, when he wasn't there constantly for her, she could find a little of his objectivity and decide for herself. After this week, maybe, just maybe she could make the kind of commitment he wanted. For now, she would explore these new realizations.

His soft breathing changed, and she knew he was awake. "Good morning," she murmured, her voice thick with sleep.

"Good morning, love." His hand stroked her naked thigh. "Want some breakfast?"

"Yuck. Just coffee." Her fingers tangled in the hair on his chest. "Later. We have plenty of time before the party." She turned her head and flicked her tongue over his hard nipple.

He groaned but attempted to keep his tone steady. "So, are you going to weasel out of this?"

"You're so suspicious," she murmured. "This night counted. And I'm not going to let you forget it."

His hand clenched convulsively. "I'm a dead man," he whispered.

A long time later, Charly and J.D. stood on her deck, frowning at a mountain of sodas and chips. "I forgot something," she said. "I always forget something. I just can't figure out what it is."

Aaron glanced up from his task of setting up another table. "Beer."

She gave him a withering glare. "These are high school students, idiot. Not even for you would I risk it."

He shrugged, grinning. "I was kidding. Loosen up."

"Charity!" called Julia from inside the house. "Do you have a chafing dish?"

"She must be joking," Charly murmured, and hurried inside.

"Julia made chicken enchiladas," Aaron said as he stood. "She had a craving at three o'clock this morning for jalapeños." He brushed off his hands and eyed J.D.'s jeans and red sports shirt reflectively. "Charly wasn't here."

"That's because she was with me." J.D. didn't flinch at Aaron's appraisal, and he was surprised when the other man's face split in a wide grin.

"I don't know what she sees in you," Aaron admitted. "But I've never had much to say about it anyway. She's always plowed her own way, ever since she was old enough to walk. We always looked for different things out of life. If that judge hadn't sent me into the army, I'd probably be in prison. Not Charly. In spite of her big talk, Charly has always had our mother's rigid morality, and her big heart. I don't." His smile froze. "She's happier than I've ever seen her right now. If you hurt her, I'll kill you."

"I could say the same for you," J.D. told him without blinking. "You mean a lot to her, and you have a lot more sway than you think. You could probably interfere." He raised one brow, and his eyes hardened. "But you won't."

Aaron stared at him a moment, then leaned back on his heels, crossing his massive arms over his chest. "No, I won't."

"Good." J.D. turned away, picked up a bag of ice, and dumped it into the plastic trash can they had designated for the soda.

He heard Aaron's chuckle behind him. "I don't know who I pity more," he murmured, then went into the house.

J.D. smiled lopsidedly and finished his task.

Hours later, as the sun reached its zenith, the house swarmed with people. The entire team, Rucker's Wolverines, filled it with noisy talk and friendly arguing. David was there, along with several other members of the staff whom J.D. hadn't met. Charly circulated from bunch to bunch, tossing a comment here, telling a joke there. J.D. mingled, but remained detached from most of the proceedings. Pride filled him as he watched Charly flitting around like an iron butterfly. If tempers suddenly ran high, she was there, with a hand on each of the antagonists, chiding and kidding them into better humor. She was magnificent.

She had changed into a green shirt that said simply GO WOLVERINES and her "good" jeans—the ones without the patches. J.D. missed those patches.

He managed to corner her by the soda, long enough to run his hand over the soft fabric at her bottom. Her blue eyes darkened for a moment, promising things to come, and she kissed him swiftly before disappearing into a knot of huge teenagers. They smiled and joked with him almost as easily as they did with Charly. He couldn't remember when anything had given him such a feeling of accomplishment. He had become a part of their group, and it felt good to belong.

She smiled brightly at him as she emerged and moved to another group. He watched her go with a little catch in his throat. No fear, no regrets, shadowed her features. Aaron was right. Charly was happier than he'd ever seen her too. She was in her element. He could never take this away from her.

But why did he have to? Why had he always thought in terms of her moving to San Francisco? The bank practically ran itself, and whatever work needed to be done he could do by modem, as he had for the last two weeks! With a few trips up a month, he could easily take care of business from here!

"Mr. Smith?" David Bakker moved beside him and offered him a soda. "Peace offering. I think I was a little pushy the last time I saw you."

J.D. accepted the drink. "It's J.D., and you've been studiously avoiding us ever since. That's not necessary."

David stroked his beard. "Maybe not. But every time I see you, all I can think of is my project." He shrugged. "I know. Egotistical."

"Not at all. It's a worthy cause."

David hesitated. "Do you know anyone else who might fund it?"

"I'm not sure." With a start, J.D. realized he no longer felt the irritation that had beset him every time that project had been mentioned in the past. It really hadn't been the thing itself, but the presentation. David had an ambitious concept, but it had lacked organization. That wasn't the fault of the proposal, but of the person who had designed it.

He had met so many of the people this man was trying to help, and he liked most of them. He thought of Hogan's mural, of Melissa's troubled love life, of the parents of some of the players he had occasionally met. They were good people. Charly's mother had been one of them, as was Charly herself. Though she lived outside the neighborhood, he knew it was her way of distancing herself, of striking a balance between what she had been and what she had become. But in the long run, she involved herself. At a grass roots level, as with her bulldozing the shacks and coaching the football team, she was the basis of everything this man stood for.

And he realized something else. David Bakker's community consolidation plan had become important to him. Oh, sure, there were some holes in it, but nothing a little work and a few amendments couldn't fix. All of the things he had mentioned to Charly that first night, the job training program, the illiteracy battle, everything could be worked in at a very small cost, if it was done correctly. All it took was the right administrator.

Suddenly that sounded quite appealing.

"Mr. Bakker," J.D. said with a grin, "I think we need to talk."

Charly scanned the deck for a sign of J.D., but he had disappeared. Frowning, she walked to the railing and searched the beach. Two figures, heads close together, strolled near the breaker line. Apprehension tickled her spine as she recognized David's massive form and J.D.'s leaner, athletic one. She remembered her night with J.D., her vehemence in defending David's project, and realized she'd nearly forgotten the whole thing. J.D. had filled her heart, her mind, her soul, to overflowing. But she wanted them to be friends, not wary opponents. If this project stood between two of the most important men in her life, she didn't know what she'd do.

"Excuse me," came a voice from behind her. "Are you Charly?"

She turned to a small, white-haired woman dressed in emerald silk. Two diamonds the size of her thumbnails adorned the woman's earlobes. Charly blinked, then recognized her. "Mrs. Smith!" She glanced down the beach, then back. "J.D. is—"

"I'm not looking for my son. Actually, I wanted to see you for myself, to evaluate your suitability." Her eyes, the exact shade of J.D.'s, raked over her, one brow raised in haughty appraisal. "I don't think we were ever properly introduced." A cool smile touched her lips as she extended a limp hand. "I remember you now, of course. You're the"—her nostrils flared delicately—"football coach."

Feeling a bubble of amusement rise in her throat, Charly took the proffered hand. "And you're the bane of J.D.'s existence," she said solemnly. "How are you?"

"I'm quite well, thank you."

"I'm glad to hear it. And how is the General? Unfurled any good parachutes lately?"

"Not recently, no."

"Oh, that's too bad. J.D. and I were just discussing skydiving the other day. I think he should take the plunge, don't you?" Charly raised both brows in polite inquiry. "Would you like a soda?"

"Ms. Czerniowski, my son is quite besotted with you, and . . . I think . . ." Amanda gave up. A huge, slow smile creased her face. "I'd love a soda." Chuckling, she extended her hand again, her grip warm and strong. "Welcome to the asylum, dear."

Exhilaration filled J.D. as he watched David return to the party. A new challenge awaited him, a new horizon beckoned. Nothing, he decided, had affected him like this since his father had died.

Though the details still had to be ironed out, David enthusiastically approved of J.D.'s plans. In fact, he'd seemed relieved. He'd had no idea that his simple idea would become so complicated. Like Charly,

David preferred the day-to-day interaction with the people. The paperwork, he explained, had daunted him.

A wide grin creased J.D.'s face. Paperwork had never daunted him.

A shout brought him out of his musings. Down the beach, Aaron stood with a football in his hand, surrounded by most of the team. With a wry chuckle he drew back his arm and burned one over to J.D., who caught it with ease. Aaron nodded his approval. "We're setting up a little impromptu game," he called. "We need another player!"

J.D. glanced toward Charly's house, then arced a steady pass right into Aaron's hands.

"Rippin'!" Hogan exclaimed. "All right! He's mine!"

"Later," J.D. told them, feeling a warm acceptance into their group. "I have to talk to Charly first."

Aaron waved him away and set up the teams.

J.D. strode to the deck, whistling a silly tune. His green eyes scanned the patio as he climbed the stairs. He wanted to share his excitement with Charly, to run up behind her and give her the biggest bear hug in the world, to tell her he loved her and to hell with her fears. Everything would be perfect.

He saw her distinctive, voluptuous backside by the hydrangeas, and his eyes narrowed in playful thought. Maybe he should pinch her instead, to pay her back for the incident on the beach. The corner of his mouth lifted, and he stalked forward.

Charly shifted a bit, and he noticed another person. Amanda!

He froze. What in the world could his mother want here?

Never mind, he thought, nothing was going to ruin his surprise. He walked forward and kissed the nape of Charly's neck. She turned, startled, then her blue eyes warmed. "I was wondering where you'd gone off to. What's up? David tore through here a minute ago, asking for the phone."

"I'll tell you in a minute." J.D. eyed Amanda warily. "The matron armor, Mother?"

"Hello to you, too, dear. What a wonderful party. I never realized before how . . . masculine football players were. Maybe I should dump the General and go after Roger Staubach."

"Amanda! I'm surprised at you." Charly grinned. "He's married."

Amanda sighed. "I suppose I should warn his wife, then." With a happy wave, she wandered off to watch the game on the beach.

"Your mother is something," said Charly.

J.D. frowned. "Yeah. But what?"

"Hey, don't do that. Don't freeze up on me. I thought that poker face of yours was gone forever." She snaked her arms around him and pulled him into the bushes. "Besides, everyone else is occupied . . ." Her mouth claimed his.

Heat rose in his loins, his niggling suspicion at Amanda's presence forgotten. Charly's teeth nibbled his lips, her tongue caressed his. J.D. pressed her to the length of his body, his palms on her bottom. She moaned and pulled him closer.

With a groan, J.D. broke the kiss. "Any more of this," he said in a raspy voice, "and we'll end up on the ground."

She chuckled huskily. "Doing it in the dirt. I love it."

He took a deep breath, fighting the fire in his body, his gaze locking onto hers. "I have to tell you something first."

"We could always run upstairs," she said, ignoring his words. "I don't think anyone would miss us."

Smiling gently, he stroked a strand of chestnut

hair away from her brow. "Your team would." She shrugged, a wicked glint in her eyes, but he held firm. "We need to talk."

With a sigh, Charly backed away and leaned against her house. "So talk. But make it quick. There's a bed with our name on it just a few feet away."

Crossing his arms over his chest, J.D. grinned. "You're a handful, aren't you?"

She nodded. "So you tell me."

"I'm not leaving Monterey," he said bluntly. "I've decided to stay."

Her smile faded, just for a moment. "I thought you were going to give us a little time."

"I am." Her response disturbed him, but he hid his reaction. She could see that this solution was perfection itself. "I'll have to go to San Francisco for a few weeks, to clear up some business. But I'll be down every weekend." He squared his shoulders. "I've decided to go ahead with David's community consolidation. Myself."

"You—" Her jaw dropped. "But you said—"

"Charly, it's a worthy project. And I think that with the right direction, it will benefit everyone. Not just—"

She cut off his words with an exuberant hug. "Oh, J.D." Her voice broke. "I love you."

Startled, he held her tightly. "I love you too." Her stranglehold increased, confusing him. "Hey, what's wrong?"

"I thought I'd have to choose," she whispered into his hair. "But you changed your mind." She kissed his ear. "You changed your mind."

"Choose?" His head whirled. His mother's presence, Charly's words, her determination of that first night, which had conveniently disappeared, his conviction that she was a worthy opponent . . . *Love is a trap, J.D.*

It was perfect, all right. Too perfect. The walls closed around him with a clang, suffocating him.

He stiffened, fighting his doubt. But Charly, sensing his withdrawal, pulled away. Her misty blue eyes stabbed his soul. She wasn't lying, he told himself. Her vulnerability was real because she had never shown it to anyone but him.

Or so she'd said.

No! She was open and honest and wouldn't pull those kind of manipulative tricks on him.

Would she?

"What's wrong?" she asked. "What did I say?"

"I changed my mind," he said hollowly, struggling to find the reality.

"I know. You said that."

"No, you said that." A cold chill racked him. "You also said you wouldn't give up."

She frowned, puzzling out his meaning. Then her blue eyes flashed with fury, and she stepped back. "You think that I *planned* this?"

"I—" He knew deep down that Charly was nothing like his mother. Doubt persisted, but he forced it away. He wouldn't let her use this as another excuse to keep them apart. "No," he said gently. "I don't think that at all. I love you." He reached for her.

She flinched. "You and your suspicious little mind! I don't believe this!" She crossed her arms over her chest. "Lord, and I'd actually forgotten that whole thing." Her mouth tightened. "I changed my mind about fencing, and I didn't accuse you!"

"Charly, you don't understand."

"Then make me understand." She tossed her head, her eyes filling again. "Make me understand how you can say you love me, how you can say that means sharing and trust, and then at the first doubt, at the first bump in the road, you forget every single word you said."

His heart twisted. "Charly, I'm sorry I doubted you. I'm human!" He waved toward the beach. "I have been at the receiving end of so many plots and ploys that I had a single instant—one instant!—of suspicion. But that's all! I thought . . ." He groped for words. "I thought it was a trap." It sounded lame now, and he felt like a fool. But he couldn't erase it completely. Too many years of tricks lay behind him.

Her eyes narrowed. "When I set a trap, Mr. Smith, you'll know it. I don't plot and I don't sneak!"

"I know that."

She looked away. "I don't think you really do," she said softly, and walked off.

"Charly, I . . ."

"What?"

"I love you."

She glanced over her shoulder. "I love you too. But that's not enough, is it?" Her spine straightened. "See you next week, J.D."

He had to think, to sort through his confusing emotions. "See you," he whispered, then left.

Thirteen

J.D. checked his watch. Ten minutes until the board meeting. He fingercombed his hair and tightened the knot in his tie, sliding it back up into its original position. For days he had moved like a zombie, his mind wrestling with his doubts. He didn't want them, but they were there, and he couldn't seem to banish his demons any better than Charly had been able to banish hers.

His mouth curved in a small smile. They were quite a pair. A dragon with fears of loneliness, and a onetime knight with a suspicious mind. How could they ever get together if their pasts kept intruding?

He sighed. Reluctantly, he stood and walked to the door. Another problem, another charity to investigate, another annual report to sift through for the bank. Life went on, but it had lost its zing. He'd never realized before just how boring his life was.

Talk in the boardroom was muted, any sound swallowed by the plush carpet and high ceiling. He walked past all of the white-haired members on the way to the front of the long oak table, a part of him noticing more whispers than usual, but his mind was so preoccupied that he didn't notice the extra attendee. He dropped his file on the table, sat with a scrunchy squeak of leather, and slipped on his glasses, his gaze on the file in front of him.

"Good afternoon, gentlemen." The whispers ceased immediately. "You all have last quarter's financial statement." The quality of the silence bothered him, and he raised his head and looked down the length of the table. "Mother!" he exclaimed. His face hardened immediately, his emotions hidden.

"Good afternoon, dear. About this statement—"

"I thought you'd sworn off these meetings."

"I had a premonition, dear. That you may need me."

He eyed her suspiciously, but she owned the place, after all, and he could hardly throw her out because of a personal problem. Turning back to the business at hand, he noticed several of the rather conservative board members darting uneasy glances at his mother, then around the room as if expecting something to pop out of the wainscoting. He didn't blame them. She had pulled a couple of rather embarrassing practical jokes during his father's reign. However, she seemed to be on her best behavior and asked several astute questions to clarify murky points.

He relaxed, as much as was possible around Amanda, and concentrated on the reports. Unfortunately, his sharp and very active mind still worked on the problem of Charly even as he proceeded with the meeting. He missed her, but couldn't get rid of his doubts. And she was right. Until he could banish those, they had no chance.

Only his mother noticed any problem with his concentration, and she smiled secretly when the someone entered the room.

"Mr. Smith?" a messenger inquired politely.

J.D. frowned at the interruption, although special

messengers weren't that unusual, even at board meetings. But this one was dressed in a trench coat and he heard a faint tinkling when she walked. It must have fogged up again outside, he thought as he identified himself. And she probably wore lots of jewelry. She did have some rather strange earrings.

"I have a special delivery, Mr. Smith," she said with a smile, and pressed the play button on the small cassette player she set before him. Wondering who could possibly have sent a recording, he almost didn't see her trench coat drop to the floor. His mind registered that she was covered in colorful silk and gold coins just as the sitar music began on the tape. Finger cymbals chimed as she swirled to start her dance, the scarves floating around her in a blinding rainbow, the dim light winking off the ruby in her navel.

"Mother!" His voice shook as he fought to control his rage.

"She's not mine. I swear!" Amanda choked on her laughter as the belly dancer draped a veil over an apoplectic board member.

Amanda was a lot of things, but she rarely swore, and he believed her. "Then who—" He watched as yet another veil came off. "Why did you come in today, Mother? And don't give me that song and dance about premonitions." Another veil came off. He wondered how anybody could make her navel jump that way without moving her hips.

Amanda applauded a particularly intricate move, and another veil fell off. "She's very good," she commented without answering.

J.D.'s eyes narrowed as the "messenger" undulated over to him. Only one other person would have done this.

A key hung from the woman's golden brassiere. Since her anatomy continued to ripple before him, he calmly reached up and tugged. It had been held in place by a tag tucked into her costume, and it came free easily. Unfortunately, her back was turned to most of the audience and he heard several gasps as he seemingly jerked at her bra. When she turned back, one gentleman nearly fainted. He got the next veil.

J.D. frowned over the key, which had a hotel's name and room number clearly stamped on it. He studied the tag. It contained only one word. "Call!"

Amusement, exasperation, exhilaration, and anger all warred inside him. A call, as she well knew, was the way fencers checked their balance. He was going to strangle her with his bare hands.

"Mother, take over!"

"Yes, dear," she said calmly. "Take as long as you need."

"Bet on it." He stripped off his glasses and dropped them in her lap, a devilish gleam in his eyes. "I'll get you for this, Mother. I don't know how, yet, but I will."

"Make me a grandmother," she said placidly. "That's punishment enough."

He strode from the room, pausing in the doorway long enough to see another veil come off. There were only two left. This would be one board meeting not soon forgotten.

"Wait'll I get my hands on you!" he muttered to an absent Charly, and the thought gave him excruciating pleasure.

Charly checked her travel clock for the thousandth time and threw a harried glance at the sinking sun outside the window. Where could he be? The girl should have delivered the key by now! She checked the clock again and growled.

Her trailing sleeve caught on the cable box on top of the TV, and she tugged at the diaphanous material impatiently. A glance in the mirror showed her brown curls were going limp. She picked up the champagne and let it slop back into its bucket of what used to be ice. Even the strawberries were warm. Her perfect sedution scene, complete with black negligee, was ruined. Had she miscalculated the time? Or something else?

Her laughter was halfhearted, and there was a bit of a hiccup at the end as she fought her tears. It would be nice to assume the messenger had gone astray, but the plain fact was that J.D. was obviously too angry. She grabbed her hairbrush and dragged it roughly through the fading curls, cursing her own stupidity. This was a rotten idea! Prodding him was hardly the way to quell his suspicions.

Her eye caught the bottle of champagne. "What the heck," she muttered, and wrestled with the cork. It shot across the room, denting a lampshade. She raised the bottle in a silent toast, then took a long pull and wiped her mouth with the back of her hand. The warm champagne bubbled out, dripping to the carpet. She set the bottle down, calmly stripped off the sheer robe, and dropped it onto the puddle, then stepped on it. The next time she left her mouth over the lip of the bottle to catch the bubbles.

A knock sounded at the door. Her heartbeat went into overdrive, and she leapt for the knob, swallowing her mouthfull so quickly, she choked. Then she realized what she wore, and fearing it was room service, she snatched the sheet from the bed and spun into it. Clearing her throat, she flung open the door. The blushing teen on the other side stood perfectly still, holding out a small, wrapped package.

"Thank you," she said, taking the package, He dropped his hand in relief.

"You're welcome." He tipped his cap and walked off.

She chuckled. He'd tipped his hat. How cute.

Puzzled, she balanced the package in her hand as she closed the door. It was small but heavy for its size. The card taped to the top said simply REVENGE? Intrigued, she tore the paper off and gaped at the figurine she'd uncovered.

It was pewter, the size of her fist—a lounging dragon with a bulging belly, tail in the air. It lay on top of a bannered helm, which read DRAGONSLAYER. A knight's gauntlet hung on the upright tail, and it was picking its teeth with a sword, obviously sated from its repast.

"Oh my Lord!" she said, two enormous tears dripping down her face. So this was why J.D. was late! The worm had turned. Damn his pointy little ears!

A loud, confident knock startled her. She set the figurine down and opened the door.

Her eyes widened. A huge bouquet of snapdragons and roses seemed suspended atop a pair of long legs before her. A ribbon stretched across the blossoms. YOU WERE RIGHT, it read. I KNEW IT.

"I love the Greek look, Athena," came a familiar, husky voice. "Or is it Egyptian?"

"You're a rat, J.D.," she whispered, her voice catching in her throat.

"I know, but I'm a cute rat." He peered around the flowers. "May I come in or should I make a horrible scene in the hall?"

"Heaven forbid that we make a scene." She chuckled weakly and waved him in. She watched as he laid the flowers on the dresser, and her heart skipped a beat as she noticed his trembling hands.

"You sure know how to telegraph a punch," he said.

"That's the only way I know."

"I know that now. And I'm sorry I ever doubted you."

"Me too."

"I'm pond scum," he said.

"Worse." Her lip quivered. "You're navel lint."

"Field droppings."

"The stuff that gets on your toes when—"

His shoulders shook. "Are we going to stand around all day degrading my character, or are we going to get married?"

The world stopped. "On two conditions," she whispered hoarsely.

He froze. "Which are?"

"Don't ever jump to conclusions."

"As long as you do the same."

"Agreed."

"And the second?"

She smiled. "Teach me to use a saber?"

"Agreed."

"In that case"—Charly toddled to him and lifted her hands to his chest—"you just try to keep me from that altar!" Her hands inched up farther, but he needed no inducement and lowered his mouth to hers, joyfully sealing the vow. Passion flared like wildfire in their veins, but he broke the kiss.

"Did you miss me as much as I missed you?"

She nodded. "And I didn't fall apart either."

"No. You never will."

"I know that now too. I can handle anything that comes my way. Most of the time." Despite her vow not to cry, her eyes filled with tears. "I'll be depending on an occasional shoulder to lean on. Or a workout."

"You'll always have it, love. Always." He pulled back and frowned at her attire. "I have to see what's under this." He tugged and unwound her. "I feel as though it's Christmas—oh!" His eyes darkened when he saw the sheer black teddy she wore. "Holy—"

"It has little pink ribbons up the sides," she pointed out, forcing herself to respond playfully. It wasn't easy when her entire body was tingling in anticipation.

"I see that," he muttered. "They're beautiful."

"Thank you." Her hands moved to his jacket, stripping it away, then began on his vest and shirt. "They untie, you know."

"No, I didn't," he said with a moan, burying his face in her hair. "But I'm dying to find out . . ."

She spun out of reach, her laughter bubbling past her lips faster than the warm champagne. "Only if you catch me!"

"Charly!" he cried. "What are you up to?"

"The final lesson?" she asked impishly, her breathing growing ragged as he finished unbuttoning his shirt and stripped it off.

He held her gaze as he slipped off his shoes.

She gulped, her body responding with fiery intensity.

He paced slowly forward, his hand on his belt as he unbuckled it. Then he lunged, but only caught the trailing edge of one of the ribbons as she skipped back, laughing again. Oh, Lord, how he'd missed that twinkle! He caught another ribbon before she made it to the other side of the room. Her left side was now exposed past her waist. This was the Charly of his dreams, the playful seductress.

"Maybe you're too encumbered," she said, snickering.

"Maybe," he commented thoughtfully, and peeled off his slacks and socks. "I feel like an idiot," he muttered, but laughed softly.

"You look wonderful," she said, her eyes searing his body with blue fire. "You are everything I've ever wanted."

"And you are everything I never expected." He groaned, his heartbeat erratic.

This time he managed both ribbons on the right before she got away. He chased her around the room, and he expected their foolish game to cool his passion. But amazingly, it fed the fire inside him. She was a tantalizing imp, an enchanting Amazon, all rolled into one. Then he cornered her, and his hand reached out to the last ribbon, the one that held the material over her breasts. "You let me catch you," he whispered accusingly.

"Revenge is sweet," she murmured as the pink satin ribbon slipped into his hand and the black lace fell away.

In the wee hours of the morning, between the words of love and commitment, Charly asked suddenly, "Why did we have to begin with foils anyway? They bend. Why couldn't we *start* with sabers, or even épées?"

J.D. chuckled softly. "Each is slightly different in their styles. Besides, you can only fence in competition with foils."

"You use sabers. You told me so."

He hesitated. "I can compete in all three. Uh, the choice is limited for . . . for women."

Taut silence reigned for two full minutes.

"We'll see about that," Charly murmured.

THE EDITOR'S CORNER

We've selected six LOVESWEPTs for next month that we feel sure will add to your joy and excitement as you rush into the holiday season.

The marvelously witty Billie Green leads off next month with a real sizzler, **BAD FOR EACH OTHER**, LOVESWEPT #372. Just picture yourself as lovely auburn-haired journalist Keely Durant. And imagine that your boss assigns you to interview an unbelievably attractive actor-musician, a man who makes millions of women swoon, Dylan Tate. Sounds fascinating, doesn't it? So why would the news of this assignment leave Keely on the verge of a collapse? Because five years before she and Dylan had been madly, wildly attracted to each other and had shared a white-hot love affair. Now, at their first reunion, the embers of passion glow and are quickly fanned to blazing flames, fed by sweet longing. But the haunting question remains: Is this glorious couple doomed to relive their past?

Please give a big and rousing welcome to brand-new author Joyce Anglin and her first LOVESWEPT #373, **FEELING THE FLAME**—a romance that delivers all its title promises! Joyce's hero, Mr. Tall, Dark, and Mysterious, was as charming to gorgeous Jordan Donner as he was thrilling to look at. He was also humorous. He was also supremely sexy. And, as it turned out, his name was Nicholas Estevis, and he was Jordan's new boss. Initially, she could manage to ignore his attractiveness, while vowing never to mix business with pleasure. But soon Nick shattered her defenses, claiming her body and soul. Passionate and apparently caring as he was, Jordan still suspected that love was a word only she used about their relationship. Would she ever hear him say the cherished word to her?

Sandra Chastain, that lovely lady from the land of moonlight and magnolias, seems to live and breathe

(continued)

romance. Next, in LOVESWEPT #374, **PENT-HOUSE SUITE,** Sandra is at her romantic Southern best creating two memorable lovers. At first they seem to be worlds apart in temperament. Kate Weston is a feisty gal who has vowed to fill her life with adventure upon adventure and never to stay put in one place for long. Max Sorrenson, a hunk with a bad-boy grin, has built a world for himself that is more safe than thrilling. When Kate and Max fall in love despite themselves, they make fireworks . . . while discovering that building a bridge to link their lives may be the greatest fun of all.

If ever there was a title that made me want to beg, borrow, or steal a book, it's Patt Bucheister's **ONCE BURNED, TWICE AS HOT,** LOVESWEPT #375. Rhys Jones, a good-looking, smooth operator, comes to exotic Hawaii in search of a mysterious woman. At first he doesn't guess that the strawberry blonde he bumped into is more than temptation in the flesh. She is part of what has brought him all the way from London. But more, the exquisite blonde is Lani . . . and she is as swept away by Rhys as he is by her. She soon learns that Rhys is everything she ever wanted, but will he threaten her happiness by forcing her to leave the world she loves?

Welcome back the handsome hunk who has been the subject of so many of your letters— *Kyle Surprise*. Here he comes in Deborah Smith's **SARA'S SURPRISE,** LOVESWEPT #376. Dr. Sara Scarborough saw that Kyle had gotten through the sophisticated security system that guarded her privacy. And she saw, of course, the terrible scars that he had brought back from their hellish imprisonment in Surador. Sara, too, had brought back wounds, the sort that stay buried inside the heart and mind. Demanding, determined, Kyle is soon close to Sara once more, close as they'd been in

(continued)

the prison. Yet now she has a "surprise" that could leave him breathless . . . just as breathless as the searing, elemental passion they share.

From first meeting—oops, make that impact—the lovers are charmed and charming in Judy Gill's thrilling **GOLDEN SWAN,** LOVESWEPT #377. Heroine B. J. Gray is one lady who is dynamite. Hero Cal Mixall is virile, dashing, and impossibly attracted to B.J. But suddenly, after reacting wildly to Cal's potent kisses, she realizes this is the man she's hated since she was a teenager and he'd laughed at her. Still, B.J. craves the sweet heat of him, even as she fears he'll remember the secret of her past. And Cal fears he has a job that is too tall an order: To convince B.J. to see herself as he sees her, as an alluring beauty. An unforgettable love story!

Do turn the page and enjoy our new feature that accompanies the Editor's Corner, our Fan of the Month. We think you'll enjoy getting acquainted with Patti Herwick.

As always at this season, we send you the same wishes. May your New Year be filled with all the best things in life—the company of good friends and family, peace and prosperity, and, of course, love. Warm wishes from all of us at LOVESWEPT.

Sincerely,

Carolyn Nichols

Carolyn Nichols
Editor
LOVESWEPT
Bantam Books
666 Fifth Avenue
New York, NY 10103

FAN OF THE MONTH

Patti Herwick

I first heard of LOVESWEPTs in a letter from Kay Hooper. We had been corresponding for some time when Kay told me she was going to start writing for Bantam LOVESWEPT. Naturally, since Kay was special—and still is—I was eager for the LOVESWEPTs to be published. I was hooked from then on. I read books for enjoyment. When a book comes complete with humor *and* a good story, I will buy it every time. As far as I'm concerned, LOVESWEPTs haven't ever changed. The outstanding authors that LOVESWEPT has under contract keep giving us readers better and more interesting stories. I am enchanted with the fantasy stories that Iris Johansen writes, the wonderful, happy stories that Joan Elliott Pickart writes, and, of course, Kay Hooper's. I can't say enough about Kay's work. She is a genius, her writing has gotten better and better. Every one of her books leaves me breathless. Sandra Brown is my favorite when it comes to sensual books, and I enjoy Fayrene Preston's books also. The fact that LOVESWEPTs are so innovative—with books like the Delaney series and Cherokee series—is another reason I enjoy reading LOVESWEPTs. I *like* different stories.

Now, as for me, I'm 44 years old, married, and have one grandchild. I think that I've been reading since the cradle! I like historical romances along with the LOVESWEPTs, and I probably read between 30 and 40 books a month. I became the proud owner of my own bookstore mostly because my husband said if I didn't do *something* about all my books, we were going to have to quit renting our upstairs apartment and let the books take over completely! I enjoy meeting other people who like to read, and I encourage my customers to talk about their likes and dislikes in the books. I never go *anywhere* without a book, and this has caused some problems. One time, while floating and reading happily on a swim mat in the water, I floated away. My husband got worried, searched, and when he found me and brought me back, he decided to do something so he wouldn't have the same problem again. Now he puts a soft nylon rope around the inflatable raft and *ties* it to the dock! I can only float 50 feet in any direction, but I can read to my heart's content.

I would like to thank LOVESWEPT for this wonderful honor. To have been asked to be a Fan of the Month is a memory I will treasure forever.

60 Minutes to a Better, More Beautiful You!

Now it's easier than ever to awaken your sensuality, stay slim forever—even make yourself irresistible. With Bantam's bestselling subliminal audio tapes, you're only 60 minutes away from a better, more beautiful you!

__	45004-2	**Slim Forever**	$8.95
__	45112-X	**Awaken Your Sensuality**	$7.95
__	45081-6	**You're Irresistible**	$7.95
__	45035-2	**Stop Smoking Forever**	$8.95
__	45130-8	**Develop Your Intuition**	$7.95
__	45022-0	**Positively Change Your Life**	$8.95
__	45154-5	**Get What You Want**	$7.95
__	45041-7	**Stress Free Forever**	$7.95
__	45106-5	**Get a Good Night's Sleep**	$7.95
__	45094-8	**Improve Your Concentration**	$7.95
__	45172-3	**Develop A Perfect Memory**	$8.95

Bantam Books, Dept. LT, 414 East Golf Road, Des Plaines, IL 60016

Please send me the items I have checked above. I am enclosing $_____ (please add $2.00 to cover postage and handling). Send check or money order, no cash or C.O.D.s please. (Tape offer good in USA only.)

Mr/Ms _____

Address _____

City/State_____ Zip_____

LT-12/89

Please allow four to six weeks for delivery.
Prices and availability subject to change without notice.

NEW!

Handsome Book Covers Specially Designed To Fit Loveswept Books

Our new French Calf Vinyl book covers come in a set of three great colors—royal blue, scarlet red and kachina green.

Each 7" × 9½" book cover has two deep vertical pockets, a handy sewn-in bookmark, and is soil and scratch resistant.

To order your set, use the form below.

ORDER FORM

STX

YES! Please send me

_____ set(s) of three book covers at $5.95 per set. Enclosed is my check/money order for the full amount. (Price includes postage and handling; NY and IL residents, please add appropriate sales tax.)   09605

Ship To:

Name	(Please Print)

Address

City	State	Zip

Send Order To: Bantam Books, Merchandise Division
P.O. Box 956
Hicksville, NY 11802

Prices in U.S. dollars

Satisfaction Guaranteed
STX—3/87

THE DELANEY DYNASTY

Men and women whose loves an passions are so glorious
it takes many great romance novels by three bestselling
authors to tell their tempestuous stories.

THE SHAMROCK TRINITY

☐	21975	**RAFE, THE MAVERICK** *by Kay Hooper*	$2.95
☐	21976	**YORK, THE RENEGADE** *by Iris Johansen*	$2.95
☐	21977	**BURKE, THE KINGPIN** *by Fayrene Preston*	$2.95

THE DELANEYS OF KILLAROO

☐	21872	**ADELAIDE, THE ENCHANTRESS** *by Kay Hooper*	$2.75
☐	21873	**MATILDA, THE ADVENTURESS** *by Iris Johansen*	$2.75
☐	21874	**SYDNEY, THE TEMPTRESS** *by Fayrene Preston*	$2.75

THE DELANEYS: *The Untamed Years*

☐	21899	GOLDEN FLAMES *by Kay Hooper*	$3.50
☐	21898	WILD SILVER *by Iris Johansen*	$3.50
☐	21897	COPPER FIRE *by Fayrene Preston*	$3.50

Buy them at your local bookstore or use this page to order.

Bantam Books, Dept. SW7, 414 East Golf Road, Des Plaines, IL 60016

Please send me the items I have checked above. I am enclosing $_____
(please add $2.00 to cover postage and handling). Send check or money
order, no cash or C.O.D.s please.

Mr/Ms _____

Address _____

City/State _____ Zip _____

SW7–11/89

Please allow four to six weeks for delivery.
Prices and availability subject to change without notice.

Special Offer
Buy a Bantam Book
for only 50¢.

Now you can have Bantam's catalog filled with hundreds of titles plus take advantage of our unique and exciting bonus book offer. A special offer which gives you the opportunity to purchase a Bantam book for only 50¢. Here's how!

By ordering any five books at the regular price per order, you can also choose any other single book listed (up to a $5.95 value) for just 50¢. Some restrictions do apply, but for further details why not send for Bantam's catalog of titles today!

Just send us your name and address and we will send you a catalog!

BANTAM BOOKS, INC.
P.O. Box 1006, South Holland, Ill. 60473

Mr./Mrs./Ms. _____
(please print)

Address _____

City _____ State _____ Zip _____

FC(A)-11/89

Please allow four to six weeks for delivery.